HAVING HER BOSS'S BABY

MAUREEN CHILD

HARLEQUIN®DESIRE

Recycling programs
for this product may
not exist in your area.

ISBN-13: 978-0-373-73403-0

Having Her Boss's Baby

Copyright © 2015 by Maureen Child

All rights reserved. Except for use in any review, the reproduction or utilization of this work in whole or in part in any form by any electronic, mechanical or other means, now known or hereinafter invented, including xerography, photocopying and recording, or in any information storage or retrieval system, is forbidden without the written permission of the publisher, Harlequin Enterprises Limited, 225 Duncan Mill Road, Don Mills, Ontario M3B 3K9, Canada.

This is a work of fiction. Names, characters, places and incidents are either the product of the author's imagination or are used fictitiously, and any resemblance to actual persons, living or dead, business establishments, events or locales is entirely coincidental.

This edition published by arrangement with Harlequin Books S.A.

For questions and comments about the quality of this book, please contact us at CustomerService@Harlequin.com.

® and TM are trademarks of Harlequin Enterprises Limited or its corporate affiliates. Trademarks indicated with ® are registered in the United States Patent and Trademark Office, the Canadian Intellectual Property Office and in other countries.

Printed in U.S.A.

HARLEQUIN®
www.Harlequin.com

Brady laughed, and the transformation was enough to take her breath away.

A handsome man when frowning, he was staggering when he smiled. "You're one of a kind, Aine. I've never met anyone quite like you."

"Thanks for that," she said, then added, "and at the risk of inflating an ego too many women before me have stroked, I'll say the same of you." She tipped her head back to meet the shadowed eyes she felt watching her with tightly restrained hunger.

He gave her a nod. "Then it's good we're not doing this."

"Absolutely. 'Tis the sensible solution."

"This is business," Brady said. "Sex would just confuse the situation."

"You're right again."

He moved in closer. "It's good we talked about it. Cleared the air. Got things settled."

"It is." She leaned toward him. "I'm sure we'll both be better off now and able to focus on our shared task."

Nodding, gaze locked with hers, he whispered, "We're not going to be sensible, are we?"

"Not at the moment, no," she said.

Then he kissed her.

* * *

Having Her Boss's Baby
is part of the Pregnant by the Boss trilogy:
Three business partners find love—and fatherhood—
where they least expect it

Dear Reader,

Having Her Boss's Baby is the first book in my Pregnant by the Boss trilogy...and oh, did I have fun. Not only did I love these characters and their story, but I was able to visit Ireland again—one of my favorite places!

Brady Finn is a man who's been alone most of his life. It's what he knows and what he's good at. Aine Donovan has never been alone. She's got family, friends and, back home in Ireland, an entire village counting on her. Brady's accustomed to giving orders and having them followed. Having Aine stand her ground and fight for what she believes in is irritating. And intriguing.

When passion explodes, leaving the two of them as unlikely prospective parents, they're going to have to find a way to compromise. But finding common ground isn't easy—even when you're in love.

I hope you'll enjoy *Having Her Boss's Baby*, and please stop by Facebook to tell me what you think! Be sure to look for the next book in this trilogy, coming in December!

Until then, I wish you good times, many laughs and, of course, wonderful books!

Maureen

Maureen Child writes for the Harlequin Desire line and can't imagine a better job. A seven-time finalist for the prestigious Romance Writers of America RITA® Award, Maureen is the author of more than one hundred romance novels. Her books regularly appear on bestseller lists and have won several awards, including a Prism Award, a National Readers' Choice Award, a Colorado Romance Writers Award of Excellence and a Golden Quill Award.

One of her books, *The Soul Collector*, was made into a CBS TV movie starring Melissa Gilbert, Bruce Greenwood and Ossie Davis. If you look closely, in the last five minutes of the movie you'll spot Maureen, who was an extra in the last scene.

Maureen believes that laughter goes hand in hand with love, so her stories are always filled with humor. The many letters she receives assure her that her readers love to laugh as much as she does. Maureen Child is a native Californian but has recently moved to the mountains of Utah.

Books by Maureen Child

Harlequin Desire

The Fiancée Caper
After Hours with Her Ex
Triple the Fun
Double the Trouble

Pregnant by the Boss trilogy
Having Her Boss's Baby

Visit the Author Profile page at Harlequin.com
or maureenchild.com for more titles.

For Bob Butler
Because we remember
And we miss you

One

Brady Finn liked his life just as it was.

So there was a part of him that was less than enthusiastic about the latest venture his company, Celtic Knot Games, was investing in. But he'd been overruled. Which was what happened when your partners were brothers who sided with each other on the big decisions even as they argued over minutiae.

Still, Brady wouldn't change a thing because the life he loved had only happened because he and the Ryan brothers had formed their company while still in college. They'd strung together their first video game with little more than dreams and the arrogance of youth.

That game, "Fate Castle," based on an ancient Irish legend, had sold well enough to finance the next game, and now Celtic Knot was at the top of the video game mountain. The three of them had already expanded their business into graphic novels and role-playing board games. Now they were moving into seriously uncharted waters.

What the hell the three of them knew about hotels could be written on the head of a pin with enough room left over for *War and Peace*. They'd drawn straws to see who would be the first of them to take over an old hotel and turn it into a fantasy. Brady had lost. He still thought the Ryans had rigged that draw to make sure he was up to bat first, but since there was nothing he could do to change the outcome he was determined to take this challenge and turn it into a win. Brady wouldn't settle for less.

The three of them had built this company from nothing. He looked around, silently approving of the workplace. Housed in a Victorian mansion on Ocean Boulevard in Long Beach, California, Celtic Knot's offices were relaxed, fun and efficient. They could have taken over a few floors of some steel-and-glass building, but none of them had liked the idea of that. Instead, they'd purchased the old house and had it rehabbed into what they needed. There was plenty of room, with none of the cold stuffiness associated with many successful companies.

There was a view of the beach from the front, and the backyard was a favorite spot for taking breaks. It was more than a place to work. It was home. The first real home he'd ever had. A home Brady shared with the only family he'd ever known.

"The designs for the new game are brilliant," Mike Ryan insisted, his voice rising as he tried to get through to his younger brother.

"Yeah, for a fifth-grade art fair," Sean countered and reached for one of the drawings scattered across the conference table to emphasize his point. "Peter's had three months to do the new storyboards. He emailed these to me yesterday as an example of what he's got for us." Clearly disgusted, he stabbed the picture with his index finger. "Take a look at that banshee," he said. "Does that look scary to you? Looks more like an underfed surfer than a servant of death."

"You're nit-picking," Mike said, shuffling through the drawings himself until he found the one he wanted. Sliding the artwork depicting a medieval hunter across the table, he said, "This is great. So he's having trouble with the banshee. He'll get it right eventually."

"That's the problem with Peter," Brady spoke up quietly, and both of the brothers turned to look at him. "It's always *eventually*. He hasn't made one deadline since he started with us."

Shaking his head, Brady reached for his coffee, which was already going cold in the heavy ceramic mug. Taking a sip, he listened as Sean said, "Agreed. We've given Peter plenty of chances to prove he's worth the money we're paying him and he hasn't done it yet. I want to give Jenny Marshall a shot at the storyboards."

"Marshall?" Mike frowned as he tried to put a face to the name.

"You know her work," Brady said. "Graphic artist. Been here about six months. Did the background art on 'Forest Run.' She's talented. Deserves the shot."

Frowning, Mike mumbled, "Okay, yeah. I remember her work on that game. But she was backup. You really think she's ready to be the lead artist?"

Sean started to speak, but Brady held up a hand. If the brothers went at it again, this argument could go on forever. "Yeah, I do. But before we do anything permanent, I'll talk to Peter. His latest deadline is tomorrow. If he fails again, that's it. Agreed?"

"Absolutely," Sean said and shot a look at his brother.

"Agreed." Mike nodded, then leaned back in his chair, propping his feet up on the corner of the table. "Now, on another topic, when's our Irish visitor arriving?"

Brady frowned. Both brothers were watching him. The Ryans had black hair and blue eyes and both of them stood well over six feet, just like Brady. They were as close as family, he reminded himself, and he was grateful for both of them—even when they irritated the hell out of him.

He stared at the older of the two brothers from across the gleaming oak conference table. "Her flight lands in an hour."

"It might've been easier for you to go to Ireland—take a look at the castle yourself."

Brady shook his head. "There's too much going on here for me to go to Europe. Besides, we've all seen the castle in the 360-degree videos."

"True," Mike said, a half smile on his face. "And it'll be perfect for our first hotel. Fate Castle."

Named after their initial success, the Irish castle would be revamped into a luxurious modern fantasy resort where guests could imagine being a part of the world that Celtic Knot had invented. Though Brady could see the potential in their expansion, he still wondered if hotels were the way to go. Then he remembered the last Comic-Con and the reaction of the fans when they'd been told about the latest idea rolling out of Celtic Knot. The place had gone nuts with cheers as their fans realized that soon they'd be able to not only visit the darkly dangerous worlds they loved but actually live in them, as well.

Brady didn't have to love the idea to see the merit in it.

"What's the woman's name again?" Sean took a seat and sprawled comfortably.

"Her last name's Donovan," Brady said. "First name, who knows? It's spelled *A-I-N-E*. Don't have a clue how to pronounce it. My best guess is *ain't* without the *T*."

"Guess it's Gaelic," Sean said, gathering up the sheaf of sketches he'd brought with him into the meeting.

"Whatever it is," Brady said, glancing down at the file they had on the castle hotel and employees, "she's been the manager for three years and by all accounts is good at her job. In spite of the fact the hotel's been losing money over the past couple of years. She's twenty-eight, degree in hotel management and lives on the property in a guest cottage with her mother and younger brother."

"She's almost thirty and still living with her mother?" Sean whistled low and long, then gave a little shudder. "Is there a picture of her in the file?"

"Yeah." He pulled it free and slid it across the table to Sean. The photo was a standard employee shot and if it was true to life, Aine Donovan wasn't going to be much of a distraction for Brady.

Which was just as well. He loved women. All women. But even if he hadn't been too busy for an affair at the moment, he had no interest in starting something up with an employee. When he wanted a woman, he had no problem finding one. But the truth was, he was happier burying himself in his work anyway. Far less aggravating to deal with the intricacies of running their company than to deal with a woman who would eventually expect more from him than he was willing to give.

Sean glanced at her photo. "She looks...*nice*."

Brady snorted at Sean's pitiful attempt to be kind.

Even he had to admit that the Irishwoman wasn't much to look at. In that photo, her hair was scraped back from her face, probably into a tidy bun. She wore glasses that made her green eyes look huge, and her pale skin looked white against the black blouse she wore buttoned primly up to the base of her throat.

"She's a hotel manager, not a model," Brady pointed out, for some reason feeling the need to defend the woman.

"Let me see that," Mike said.

Sean passed the slightly out-of-focus photo across the table. Mike studied it for a minute. Lifting his gaze to Brady's, Mike shrugged. "She looks…efficient."

Shaking his head at the two of them, Brady took the picture back, slid it into the file and closed the folder. "Doesn't matter what she looks like as long as she can do the job. And according to the reports we got on the hotel and its employees, she's good at what she does."

"Have you talked to her about the changes we've got planned?"

"Not really," he told Mike. "It was pointless to try to explain everything long distance. Besides, we only just got the finalized plan for the remodel."

Since the construction crews would begin work in a month, it was time to bring Aine Donovan up to date.

"Well, if we're finished with the Irish news," Sean said, "I had a call from a toy company interested in marketing some of our characters."

"Toys?" Mike sneered. "Not really who we are, Sean."

"Gotta agree." Brady shook his head. "Our games are more for the teenagers-and-up crowd."

"True, but if they were collectibles…" Sean's voice trailed off even as he gave them both a small smile.

Brady and Mike looked at each other and nodded.

"Collectibles is a different story," Brady said. "We get people excited about owning our characters—that will only push the games themselves higher up the food chain."

"Yeah, that could work," Mike finally said. "Get some numbers. Once we have a better idea of the licensing agreement we can talk it over again."

"Right." Sean stood up and looked at Brady. "You picking up Irish from the airport?"

"No." Brady stood, too, and gathered up the file folder. "I've got a car meeting her and taking her directly to the hotel."

"That's the personal touch," Sean muttered.

Brady snapped, "It's not a date, Sean. She's coming here to work."

"You setting her up at the Seaview?" Mike asked, interrupting Sean.

"Yeah." The company kept a suite at the nearby hotel for visiting clients. It was within walking distance to their business, which made meetings easier to arrange. It was also where Brady lived, in a penthouse suite. "I'll go over there this afternoon to meet with her. Tomorrow's soon enough for us to show her what we've got in mind for the remodel."

Once the three of them explained the situation to Aine Donovan, she could get back to Ireland and, more important, Brady could get back to his life.

"I'm here, Mum, and it's just lovely."

"Aine?"

She winced at the sleepy tone of her mother's voice. Standing on the balcony off the living room of her hotel suite, Aine stared out at the blue Pacific and finally re-membered the time difference between California and home. Here in Long Beach, it was four in the afternoon and a warm sun was shining out of a clear sky. Back in County Mayo, it was…after midnight.

Now that she thought about it, Aine realized she should be exhausted. But she wasn't. Excitement about the travel, she guessed, tangled with anxiety over what was going to happen once she met with Brady Finn about her castle. All right, not *her* castle, but certainly more hers than his, despite his having bought the place a few months ago. What did he know of its traditions, its history and legacy, its importance to the village where her friends lived? *Nothing, that's what*, she told herself, though she'd make him aware of all of it before he began whatever re-modeling he had in mind.

It worried her to be sure—what did a video game maven want with a centuries-old castle in a tiny village in Ireland? It wasn't as though Castle Butler had ever been a tourist draw. There were far finer estates, much easier to get to, dotting the Irish countryside.

Thoughts whirled in her brain, circling each other, making her mind a jumble that only cleared momen-tarily when her mother spoke again. "Aine. You've ar-rived, then?"

"I have. I'm so sorry, Mum. I completely forgot—"

"No matter." Molly Donovan's voice became clearer and Aine could almost see her mother sitting up in bed, trying to wake herself. "I'm glad you called. Your flight was all right, then?"

"More than all right." She'd never flown in a private jet before, and now that she had, Aine knew she'd never be happy in coach again. "It was like flying while relaxing in a posh living room. There were couches and tables and flowers in the loo. The flight attendant made fresh cookies," she said. "Cooked them up right there on the plane. Or maybe only heated them. But there was a real meal and champagne to go with it and really, I was almost sorry when the flight ended."

A hard truth indeed, because once her travel was over, it meant that she had no choice but to face down the man who owned the company that had the power to ruin her life and the lives of so many others. But, she argued with herself, why would he do that? Surely he wouldn't purchase the castle only to shut down the hotel? True enough that profits hadn't been what they should be in the past couple of years, but she had ideas to change all that, didn't she? The previous owner hadn't wanted to be bothered. She could only hope that this one would.

Although, she had to say, he was setting the scene perfectly to keep her off balance, wasn't he? Sending a private jet for her. Then, rather than meeting her himself, he'd had a driver there holding a sign with her name on it. Arranging for her to stay in a suite that was larger than the entire first floor of the guest cottage where she and her family lived, yet not a whisper of a personal greeting from the man.

He was letting her know, without speaking a word, that he was in charge. Master to servant, she supposed, and wondered if all exceedingly wealthy people were the same.

"It sounds lovely. And now?" her mother asked. "You're tucked into a hotel?"

"I am," Aine said, turning her face into the wind driving in from the sea. "I'm standing on a terrace looking out at the ocean. It's warm and lovely, nothing like spring at home."

"Aye," her mother agreed. "Rained all day and half the night. Now, you'll have your meeting with the new owner of the castle soon, won't you?"

"I will." Aine's stomach fluttered with the wings of what felt like a million butterflies. She laid one hand on her abdomen in a futile attempt to ease that stirring of nerves. "He's left a message for me saying he'll be here at five."

A message, she told herself and shook her head. Again, she recalled the man hadn't bothered to meet her at the airport or give her the courtesy of being here when she arrived. All small ways to impress upon her that she was on his territory now and that he would be the one making the decisions. Well, he might hold the purse strings, but she would at least be heard.

"You'll not be a terrier at the man from the beginning, will you?" her mother asked. "You'll have some patience?"

Patience was a difficult matter for Aine. Her mother had always said that Aine had been born two weeks early and hadn't stopped running since. She didn't like waiting. For anything. The past few months, knowing that the castle had been sold but having no more information beyond that, had nearly driven her around the bend. Now she wanted answers. She needed to know what the new owner of Castle Butler was planning—so she could prepare.

"I'll not say a thing until I've heard him out, and that's the best I can promise," she said and hoped she could keep that vow.

It was only that this was so important. To her. To her

family. To the village that looked to the castle's guests to shop in their stores, eat in their pubs. Now a trio of American businessmen had purchased the castle and everyone was worried about what might happen.

For the past three years, Aine had managed the castle hotel and though she'd had to fight the owner for every nail and gallon of paint needed for its upkeep, she felt she'd done a good job of it. Now though, things had changed. It wasn't only the hotel she had to see to—it was the survival of her village and her family's future she fought for. She hated feeling off balance, as if she was one step behind everyone else in the bloody world. It was being here, in California, that was throwing her. If Brady Finn had come to Ireland, she might have felt more in control of the situation. As it was, she'd have to stay on her toes and impress on the new owner the importance of the responsibility he had just acquired.

"I know you'll do what's best," her mother said.

It was hard, having the faith of everyone you knew and loved settled on your shoulders. More than her mother and brother were counting on her; the whole village was worried, and Aine was their hope. She wouldn't let them down.

"I will. You go back to sleep now, Mum. I'll call you again tomorrow." She paused and smiled. "At a better time."

Aine took the time before the arrival of her new employer to freshen up. She fixed her makeup, did her hair and, since she was running out of time, didn't bother with changing her clothes, only gave them a quick brush.

But when five o'clock came and went with still no sign of her new employer, Aine's temper spiked. So much for her vow of patience. Was he so busy, then, that he couldn't even be bothered to contact her to say his plans had changed? Or did he think so little of her that being late for their appointment didn't bother him? The phone in her suite rang and when she answered, the hotel desk clerk said, "Ms. Donovan? Your driver is here to take you to the Celtic Knot offices."

"My driver?"

"Yes. Apparently Mr. Finn was delayed and so sent a driver to take you to your meeting."

Irritation rippled along her nerve endings. In seconds, her mind raced with outraged thoughts. Hadn't she flown thousands of miles to meet with him? And now, after being ignored by the great man, she was being sent for, was she? Lord of the manor summoning a scullery maid? Had he a velvet rope in his office that he tugged on to get all of his servants moving in a timely fashion?

"Ms. Donovan?"

"Yes. I'm sorry, yes." It wasn't this man's fault, was it, that her new employer had the manners of a goat? "Would you please tell the driver I'll be down in a moment?"

She hung up, then took another moment to check her reflection. But for the anger-infused color in her cheeks, she looked fine, though she briefly considered changing her clothes after all. Aine decided against it as she doubted very much her new employer would be pleased if she kept him waiting.

Thankfully, flying on a private jet hadn't left her looking as haggard as surviving a twelve-hour flight in economy would have. So she would go now to meet the man who clearly expected his underlings to leap into motion when he spoke. And she would, even if it killed her, keep her temper.

Two

"We need the new storyboards by tomorrow afternoon at the latest," Brady barked into the phone. He'd been hung up for the past two hours with call after call and his patience was strained to the breaking point. "No more excuses, Peter. Meet the deadline or be replaced."

Artists were difficult to deal with in the best of times. But Peter Singer was an artist with no ambition and no idea of how to schedule his time. With the best of intentions, the man laid down deadlines, then because he was so disorganized, he never managed to meet the dates he himself had arranged.

His talent wasn't in question. Peter was good at sketching out the boards the programmers would use to lay out the basic story line of their newest game. And without that road map, the whole process would be brought to a crawl. In fact, Peter was good enough at his work that

Brady had given him several extensions when he'd asked for them. But he wasn't getting another one.

"Brady, I can have them for you by the end of the week," the man was arguing. "I'm on a roll here, but I can't get them by tomorrow. That's just impossible. I swear they'll be worth the wait if you—"

"Tomorrow, Peter," Brady said flatly, as he turned in his desk chair to stare out the window behind him. "Have them here by five tomorrow or start looking for another job."

"You can't rush art."

"If I can pay for it, I can rush it," Brady told him, idly watching a blackbird jump from branch to branch in the pine tree out back. "And you've had three months on your last extension to make this deadline, so no sense in complaining now that you're being rushed. Do it or not. Your choice."

He hung up before he could be drawn into more of Peter's dramatic appeals. He'd been dealing with marketing most of the day—not his favorite part of the job anyway—so he admittedly had less patience than he normally would have for Peter's latest justification for failure. But the point was, they had a business to run, schedules to keep and for the past year Peter hadn't been able to, or wasn't interested in, keeping to the schedule. It was time to move on, find another graphic artist who could do the job. Sean was right. Jenny Marshall deserved a shot.

And now, rather than head home for a well-deserved beer, Brady had one more meeting to get through. As the thought passed through his mind, he heard a brisk knock at his door and knew the Irishwoman had arrived.

"Come in."

The door opened and there she was.

Auburn hair and green eyes identified her as Aine Donovan, but there the resemblance to the woman in the employee photo ended. He'd been prepared for a spinster-ish female, a librarian type. *This* woman was a surprise.

His gaze swept her up and down in a blink, taking in everything. She wore black slacks and a crimson blouse with a short black jacket over it. Her thick dark red hair fell in heavy waves around her shoulders. Her green eyes, not hidden behind the glasses she'd worn in her photo, were artfully enhanced and shone like sunlight in a forest. She was tall and curvy enough to make a man's mouth water, and the steady, even stare she sent him told Brady that she also had strength. Nothing hotter than a gorgeous woman with a strong sense of self. Unexpectedly, he felt a punch of desire that hit him harder than anything he'd ever experienced before.

Discomfited, he tamped down that feeling instantly and fought to ignore it. Desire had its place, and this def-initely wasn't it. She worked for him, and sex with an employee only set up endless possibilities for problems. Even that fact, though, wasn't enough to kill the want that only increased the moment she opened her mouth and the music of Ireland flavored her words.

"Brady Finn?"

"That's right. Ms. Donovan?" He stood up and waited as she crossed the room to him, her right hand out-stretched. She moved with a slow, easy grace that made him think of silk sheets, moonlit nights and the soft slide of skin against skin. Damn.

"It's Aine, please."

She pronounced it *Anya* and Brady knew he never

would have figured that out from its spelling. "I wondered how to say your first name," he admitted.

For the first time, a hint of a smile touched her mouth, then slipped away again. "'Tis Gaelic."

He took her hand in his and felt a buzz of sensation shoot straight up his arm, as if he'd grabbed a live electrical wire. It was unexpected enough that he let her go instantly and just resisted rubbing his palm against his pant leg. "I assumed so. Please, have a seat."

She sat down in one of the chairs in front of his desk and slowly crossed one leg over the other. It was an unconsciously seductive move that he really resented noticing.

"How was your flight?" he blurted out, wanting to steer the conversation into the banal so his mind would have nothing else to torment him with.

"Lovely, thanks," she said shortly and lifted her chin a notch. "Is that what we're to talk about, then? My flight? My hotel? I wonder that you care what I think. Perhaps we could speak instead about the fact that twice now you've not showed the slightest interest in keeping your appointments with me."

Brady sat back, surprised at her nerve. Not many employees would risk making their new boss angry. "Twice?"

"You sent a car for me at the airport and again at the hotel." She folded her hands neatly atop her knee. If she was uneasy about speaking her mind, she didn't show it.

He merely looked at her for a long moment before saying, "Was there something wrong with the car service?"

"Not at all. But I wonder why a man who takes the trouble to fly his hotel manager halfway across the world can't be bothered to cross the street and walk a block to meet her in person."

When Brady had seen her photo, he'd thought, *Efficient, cool, dispassionate*. Now he had to revise those thoughts entirely. There was fire here, sparking in her eyes and practically humming in the air around her.

Damned if he didn't like it.

It was more than simple desire he felt now—there was respect, as well.

Which meant that he was in more trouble here than he would have thought.

Aine could have bitten her own tongue off. Hadn't she promised herself to rein in her temper? And what did she do the moment she met her new boss? Insult him was what. An apology was owed him and Aine knew it, though the words stuck in her throat and wouldn't come free. Yes, she shouldn't have spoken to him so, but nothing she'd said was untrue, was it? Oh, she should have taken a moment to calm herself before coming into his office. Instead, she'd allowed her temper to simmer into a fine boil and then spill over the moment she met the man. Now there was an unwanted tension between them and she had to find a way to try to smooth things over.

The trouble was, Aine told herself as she met his steady gaze across the wide expanse of his desk, she hadn't expected him to be so...wildly attractive. On the short ride to his office, she'd told herself to be confident. Then the door had opened and she'd taken one look at the man and gone light-headed enough that all her good intentions had simply dissolved.

His thick black hair fell across his forehead, making her want to reach out and smooth it back. His strong jaw, sharp blue eyes and just the barest hint of whiskers on his cheeks made him seem so much more than a man who made his fortune by inventing games. He looked like a pirate. A highwayman. A dark hero from one of the romance novels she loved to read. Something raw and wild in him teased to life all sorts of inappropriate thoughts in her mind and stirred something warm and wonderful through her blood.

This wasn't something she wanted, or was even interested in, she assured herself. But it seemed she had no choice but to feel that whip of heat and tendrils of desire snaking through her body. When he shook her hand, she'd wanted to hold on to that tight, firm grip just a bit longer, but she was grateful, too, when he deliberately let her go. Well, now she wasn't even making sense to herself. This was not a good sign.

Trying to distract herself, Aine admitted that not only was the man himself unexpected, but his office was, as well. She had thought to find Celtic Knot in one of those eerily modern glass-and-chrome buildings. Instead, the old home they'd transformed into a work space was both charming and surprising. And it gave her just a bit of hope for the castle—if this man's company could modernize an old building such as this and maintain its character, perhaps they could do the same with Castle Butler, too.

With that thought firmly in mind, Aine settled into the uncomfortable chair, swallowed her pride like a bitter pill and forced herself to say, "I'll apologize for biting your head off first thing."

His eyebrows arched, but he didn't speak, so Aine continued on in a rush—before he could open his mouth to say, "You're fired."

"It's the jet lag, I'm sure, that's put me in a mood." Though she wasn't at all tired, she would reach for the most understandable excuse.

"Of course," he said, though it was clear from his tone he wasn't buying that. "And I'll apologize for not meeting you personally. We're very busy right now, with one game being released this week and the next due out in December."

Games, she thought. Wasn't her younger brother, Robbie, forever playing this man's games? Ancient legends of Ireland brought to life so people around the world could pretend to be Celts fighting age-old evil. She didn't yet see why a company that built video games was buying a hotel in Ireland, though, and she was willing to admit, at least to herself, that she was worried about what might be coming.

"There isn't time enough today to get into all of our plans for the castle, but I did want to meet with you to let you know that changes are coming."

Instantly, it seemed, a ball of ice dropped into the pit of her stomach as every defensive instinct she possessed fired up. "Changes, is it?"

"You had to assume things would change, Aine." He sat forward, propping his arms on the desk, and met her gaze. "The past couple of years, your castle has been losing money."

She bristled and felt the first tremor of anxiety ripple through her. Was he saying she was at fault for the hotel losing money? Had he brought her all this way just to fire her? Was she about to lose not only her job but her home? Now it seemed she not only needed to defend her castle but herself, as well. "If you're thinking my management of the castle has been lacking—"

"Not at all," he interrupted her, and held up one hand to keep her from speaking again. "I've gone over the books, as have my partners, and we all agree that your skills are what held the place together the past couple of years."

A relieved breath escaped her, but that sensation didn't last long.

"Still," he continued, and Aine felt as though she were hypnotized. She couldn't tear her gaze from him, from his eyes. There was something pulling her toward him even as her common sense was shrieking a warning. Working with him would have been so much easier if he had been the stereotypical computer nerd—skinny, awkward. Instead, Brady Finn was obviously the kind of man who was used to issuing orders and having them obeyed without question. That worried her a bit, as she'd never been one to blindly fall in line.

"We'll be making some substantial changes both to the castle itself and the way it's run."

Well, that simple sentence sent cold chills dancing through her. "What sort of *substantial* changes did you have in mind?" The words forced their way out of her mouth.

"Time enough to get into all of that," he said and stood up. "We'll get started on it tomorrow."

Tomorrow. She was worried enough that she didn't mind putting off whatever was coming. Yet at the same time, she knew she wouldn't sleep a wink for thinking of it.

Her gaze tracked him. He was tall and broad shouldered, and in his white dress shirt his chest looked as wide as the sky. Her mouth went dry as she stood to face him. His eyes were fixed on her, and there was power in those blue depths. The kind of power only rich men knew. It was a mix of wealth and confidence and the surety of his own convictions. And that kind of man would not be easy to stand against.

"You must be hungry," he said.

"I am, a bit," she admitted, though if he continued to stare at her in just that way, she'd be lucky to swallow a single bite.

"Then, we'll go to an early dinner and talk." He walked to a closet, opened it and pulled out a black jacket. Shrugging it on, he went back to her side and waited.

"Talk?" she asked. "About what?"

He took her arm, threaded it through his and headed for the door. "You can tell me all about yourself and the castle."

She'd no interest in talking about herself, but maybe, she thought, she could impress on him what the castle meant to those who worked there and the people in the nearby village, as well.

"All right," she said, then hesitated, remembering she hadn't even changed clothes since her flight. "But I'm not dressed for it, really."

"You look great," he assured her.

How like a man was all she could think.

"If we could stop by my hotel first," she said, dismissing his words, "I'd like to change."

He shrugged and said, "Sure."

She was worth the wait, Brady thought, looking across the linen-draped tablecloth at Aine. She wore a simple black dress with wide shoulder straps and a square neckline that displayed just the hint of the tops of her breasts. Her skin glowed like fine porcelain in the candlelight, and the candle flames seemed to shoot golden sparks through her dark red hair and wink off the tiny gold stars she wore at her ears.

His insides burned, and watching her smile and sip at her wine was only stoking the flames. She was… temptation, Brady told himself. One he didn't want to resist but would have to.

"It's lovely wine," she said, setting her glass down.

"Yeah. Lovely." He didn't mean the wine and, judging by the flash in her eyes, she knew it. Damn. This upscale restaurant with the candlelight had probably been a mistake. He should have taken her for a nice casual burger in a crowded diner. This setting was too damn intimate.

The only way to keep the want clawing at him in check was to steer this conversation to business and keep it there. A shame that his brain didn't exactly have dibs on his blood supply at the moment. "Tell me about the castle. From your perspective, what needs to be done?"

She took a breath, then another sip of wine, and set the glass down again before speaking. "It's true, there does need to be some remodeling. Bathrooms updated, new paint throughout, of course, and the furniture's a bit shabby. But the building itself is strong and sure as it has been since it was first built in 1430."

Almost six hundred years. For a man with no family, no personal history to talk about, that kind of longevity seemed impossible to understand and accept. But as a man with no roots, changes came easier to him than they would to people like her. People who clung to traditions and tales of the past.

"We're going to do all of that, of course," he said. "And more."

"That's what worries me," she admitted. "The *more*. I

know you've said we'd talk about this tomorrow, but can you tell me some small things that you have in mind?"

Hard to concentrate on the conversation when listening to her speak made that twist of desire inside him curl tighter. But maybe talking about the castle would help give him something else to focus on. Deliberately, he took a gulp of his wine to give himself time to settle. When he could think clearly again, he said, "Our company, Celtic Knot, is going into the hotel business."

She nodded and waited for him to continue.

"Starting with Castle Butler, we're buying three hotels and reimagining them."

"*Reimagine* sounds much grander than a few simple changes," she said, suspicion clear in her tone.

"It is," he said. "We're going to turn them into mockups of our three bestselling games."

"Games."

Warming to his theme, Brady said, "The first will be Fate Castle."

"Fate…?"

"Designed after our first successful game."

"I know of it," she said quietly.

His eyebrows shot up, and he couldn't quite keep the surprise out of his voice when he asked, "You've played it? And here I was thinking you didn't look the gaming type to me."

"There's a type, is there?" She ran her fingers up and down the stem of her wineglass, but the movement was anything but smooth and relaxed. "As it happens, you'd be right. I don't play, but my younger brother, Robbie, does. He's mad for your games."

Brady smiled in spite of the coolness in her eyes. "He has excellent taste."

"I wouldn't know," she said with detachment, "for the idea of using a toy to chase down zombies and wraiths doesn't appeal to me."

"You shouldn't knock it until you've tried it."

"What makes you think I haven't?"

"You'd like it more if you had," he said simply. He knew their games were addictive to players. "Our games are more than just running and shooting. There are intricate puzzles to be solved. Choices made, and the player takes the consequences for those choices. Our games are more sophisticated in that we expect our players to *think*."

She smiled briefly. "To listen to Robbie shouting and railing against the game, you wouldn't know it was a test of intelligence."

He smiled again as her voice twisted the knots in his belly even tighter. "Well, even smart guys get angry when they don't succeed at first try."

"True enough," she said, then paused as the waiter delivered their meals.

La Bella Vita was Brady's favorite restaurant. Elegant, quiet, and the food was as amazing as the atmosphere. The walls were a pale yellow, with paintings of Italy dotting the space. Candles flickered atop every one of the linen-draped tables, and soft music sighed through the speakers tucked into the corners of the room. The clink of crystal and the rise and fall of muted conversations around them filled the silence while Aine took a bite of her crab-stuffed ravioli in Alfredo sauce.

"Good?" he asked.

"Wonderful," she said, then asked, "Do you often bring your employees to such a fine restaurant?"

"No," he admitted and couldn't have said, even to himself, why he'd brought Aine here. They could have stopped for a burger somewhere or eaten at the restaurant in her hotel. Instead, he'd brought her here, as if they were on a date. Which they really weren't. Best to steer this back to work. "It's quiet here, though, and I thought that would give us a chance to talk."

"About the castle."

"Yes, and about your part in helping us make this happen."

"My part?" Genuine surprise flashed in her eyes.

Brady took a bite of his own ravioli, then said, "You'll be there on-site, for the day-to-day changes. We need you to oversee the workers, make sure they stay on schedule, on budget, things like that."

"I'm to be in charge?"

"You're my liaison," he told her. "You come to me with problems, I take care of them, then you make sure they're handled right."

"I see." She dragged her fork listlessly across her plate. "Is there a problem?"

"Have you given thought to who will be doing the work?"

"We've got the best contractor in California lined up," Brady said. "He'll be bringing in crews he trusts."

She frowned a bit. "Things might go easier and more quickly if you hired Irish workmen."

"I don't like working with people I don't know," he said.

"Yet here we are, and you don't know me from the man in the moon."

"True." He nodded. "Fine. I'll think about it."

"Good. But you've yet to tell me what kind of changes you're talking about." She met his gaze. "You said only that you were going to 'reimagine' things. Which could mean anything at all. What exactly are you planning?"

"Nothing structural," he told her. "We like the look of Castle Butler—that's why we bought it. But there will be plenty of changes made to the interior."

She sighed, set her fork down and admitted, "To be honest, that's what I'm worried about."

"In what way?"

"Will I be seeing zombies in the hallways?" she asked. "Cobwebs strung across the stone?"

She looked so worried about that possibility, Brady grinned. "Tempting, but no. We'll go into all the details starting tomorrow, but I'll say tonight I think you'll like what we've got in mind."

Folding her hands on the table, she looked at him and said, "I've worked at Castle Butler since I was sixteen and went into the kitchens. I worked my way up from there, becoming first a maid, then moving on through reception and finally into managing the castle.

"I know every board that creaks, every draft that blows through broken mortar. I know every wall that needs painting and every tree in the garden that needs trimming." She paused, took a breath and continued before he could speak, "Everyone who works in the castle is a friend to me, or family. The village depends on the hotel for its livelihood and their worries are mine, as well. So," she said softly, "when you speak of reimagining the castle, know that for me, it's not about games."

Brady could see that. Her forest green eyes met his, and he read the stubborn strength in them that foretold all kinds of interesting battles ahead.

Damned if he wasn't looking forward to them.

Three

By the following day, Aine was sure she'd stepped in it with Brady at dinner. She'd had such plans to mind her temper and her words and hadn't she thrown all those plans to the wind the moment he mentioned "substantial changes"?

She sipped room-service tea and watched the play of sunlight on the water from her balcony. The tea was a misery, and why was it, she wondered, that Americans couldn't brew a decent cup of tea? But the view was breathtaking—the water sapphire blue, crested with whitecaps, and in the distance, a boat with a bright red sail skimmed that frothy surface.

She only wished the vista was enough to clear her mind of the mistakes made the night before. But as her father used to say, she'd already walked that path—it was useless to regret the footprints left behind.

So she would do better today. She'd meet Brady Finn's partners and be the very *essence* of professionalism…

Not two hours later, she felt her personal vow to maintain a quiet, dignified presence shatter like glass.

"You can't mean it."

Aine had remained silent during most of this meeting with all three partners of Celtic Knot Games. She'd listened as they'd tossed ideas back and forth, almost as if they'd forgotten her presence entirely. She'd bitten her tongue so many times, that particular organ felt swollen in her mouth. And yet, there came a time when a woman could be silent no longer and Aine had just reached it. Looking from one man to the other, she focused on Sean Ryan since he seemed to be the most reasonable.

"You're talking about turning a dignified piece of Irish history into a mockery of itself," she said bluntly.

Before Sean could speak, his brother said, "I understand you feel a little protective of the castle, but—"

"Protective, yes, but it's more than that," she argued, shifting her gaze from one to the other of the three men, ending finally by meeting Brady's gaze. "There's tradition. There's the centuries etched into every stone."

"It's a building," Brady said. "One that you yourself have already agreed needs remodeling."

"To that, yes, I do agree," she said quickly, leaning toward him a bit to emphasize what she wanted to say. "And I'm pleased to hear you're going to make some long-needed repairs to the castle. I've some ideas for changes that would enhance our guests' experiences even while keeping the building's, for lack of a better word, *soul* intact."

Amused, Brady asked, "You believe the castle has a soul?"

She looked almost affronted. "It's been standing since 1430," she reminded him, so focused on Brady alone that the other men in the room might not have been there at all. "People have come and gone, but the castle remains. It's stood against invaders, neglect and indifference. It's housed kings and peasants and everything in between. Why wouldn't it have a soul?"

"That's very…Irish of you to think so."

She didn't care for the patronizing smile he offered her. "As you're Irish yourself, you should agree."

Brady's features froze over. It was as if she'd doused him with a bucket of ice water. Aine didn't know what it was about her simple statement that had turned him to stone, but clearly, she'd hit a very sore spot.

"Only my name is Irish," he said shortly.

"An intriguing statement," she answered, never moving her gaze from his.

"I'm not trying to intrigue you," he pointed out. "I'm saying that if you're looking for a kindred spirit in this, it's not me."

"Okay," Sean said, voice overly cheerful. "So we're all Irish here—some of us more than others. Let's move on, huh?"

Aine stiffened, didn't so much as acknowledge Sean's attempt to lighten the mood. "I'm not looking for a friend or a confidante or a kindred spirit, as you say," she said and every word was measured, careful, as she deliberately tried to hold on to a temper that was nearly choking her. "I've come thousands of miles at your direction to discuss the future of Castle Butler. I can give you information on the building, the village it supports and the country it resides in. All of which you might have found out for yourself had you bothered to once visit the property in person."

Silence hummed uncomfortably in the room for a few long seconds before Brady spoke up. "While I admire your guts in speaking your mind, I also wonder if you think the wisest course of action is to piss off your new boss."

"All right, then," she forced herself to say at last. "I'll apologize for my outburst, as it wasn't my intention to insult you."

"No need to apologize."

"I'll decide for myself when I'm wrong, thanks," she said, shaking her head firmly. "I promised myself I'd keep my temper in check, and I didn't. So for that I'm sorry."

"Fine."

She swept her gaze across all three men, who were now watching her as if she was an unstable bomb. "But I won't apologize for telling you what I think about the castle and its future."

Once again, she met the eyes of all three men before focusing on Brady alone. "I've been nervous about this meeting. It's important to me that the people who work at the castle—including me—keep our jobs. I want the castle to shine again, as it should."

Brady's gaze held hers, and she felt the Ryan brothers watching her, as well. Maybe she should have kept her mouth shut. Perhaps she didn't have the right to say anything at all about their plans for the place she loved. But she couldn't sit idly by and pretend all was well when it certainly wasn't.

Still meeting Brady's gaze, she asked, "Did you bring me all this way to simply agree with your decisions? Is that what you expect from your hotel manager? To stand quietly at your side and do everything you say?"

Brady tipped his head to one side and studied her. "You're asking if I want a yes man?"

"Exactly."

"Of course I don't," he said sharply. "I want your opinions, as I told you last night."

Aine blew out a breath. "Now that you've opened the door, I can only hope you won't regret it."

"I admire honesty," he said. "Doesn't mean I'll agree with you—but I want to know what you really think about what we're planning."

Nodding, she sat more easily in her chair and glanced at the Ryan brothers. "I'll say it's hard to form an opinion with nothing more to go on than these descriptions of your ideas you've been giving me."

"I think we can take care of that," Mike said. "We've got a few drawings that could give you a better picture of what we have in mind."

Brady nodded. "Jenny Marshall's drafted some basic art that should help."

"Jenny Marshall again?" Mike looked at his brother. "What, is she our go-to artist now?"

Aine leaned back in her chair and shook her head. Watching the brothers argue, and Brady following along, was a real lesson. The three men were clearly a unit and yet Aine had the sense that Brady was still holding back, even from his friends. As if he was deliberately standing outside, looking in from a safe distance.

Even while the Ryans' heated discussion amped up, she continued to watch Brady and his reaction to his friends. He seemed completely at ease with their argument, and since the brothers were Irish, she was willing to bet their differences of opinion happened frequently. The mystery for her was why he separated himself from the disagreement. Did he simply not care one way or the other about the artist's work or was it an inborn remoteness that drove him?

"Jenny's good, I keep telling you." Sean shrugged. "You haven't even looked at the mock-ups she's done of the stuff Peter was supposed to have finished five months ago."

"It's Peter's job, not hers," Mike reminded his brother. "Why would I look at what she's doing?"

"So you could appreciate just how good she is?" Sean asked.

Mike scowled at his younger brother. "Why are you so anxious to push Jenny off on us?"

"He just told you why," a voice said as the door opened to admit a petite, curvy woman with short, curly blond hair. Her blue eyes narrowed on Mike Ryan briefly before she looked at Sean and smiled. Crossing the room, she handed him a large black portfolio. "Sorry this took longer than I thought, but I wanted to finalize a few details this morning before bringing them to you."

"No problem, Jenny, thanks."

While sunlight slanted through the wide windows, Jenny and Mike faced each other across the conference table. Aine watched the byplay between the tiny blonde and the older of the Ryan brothers. There was a near visible tension humming in the room as the two of them glared at each other. And yet, she thought, neither of the other men in the room seemed to notice.

In fact, Brady and Sean were so fixed on the portfolio, they never saw the blonde sneer at Mike Ryan before slipping from the room and closing the door quietly behind her. Clearly, Jenny Marshall wasn't afraid to stand up for herself, and though Aine didn't know the woman at all, she felt a kinship with her.

"What the hell, Sean," Mike muttered when she was gone. "You could have told me she was coming in this morning."

"Why? So we could argue about it?" Sean shook his head and spread the series of drawings across the table. "This way was easier. Just take a look, will you?"

Aine was already looking, coming to her feet so she could see every one of the drawings Jenny had brought in. Sean was right about the woman being a wonderful artist. There was real imagination and brilliance in the artwork, whether Aine liked the subject matter or not. She recognized Castle Butler, of course, but the images she was looking at were so different from the place she'd left only a day or two before, it was hard to reconcile them.

"Okay, yeah, they're good," Mike said shortly.

"Wow," Sean said. "Quite the concession."

"Shut up," his brother retorted. "This still doesn't say she should be doing Peter's job."

"It really does," Brady put in, using his index finger to drag a rendering of the castle's main hall closer toward him. "I haven't seen Peter do work like this in, well…ever."

"There you go!" Sean slapped Brady on the back and gave an I-told-you-so look to his brother. "We promote Jenny to lead artist and we'll get back on track and stay there."

"I don't know…" Mike shook his head.

"What do you need to be convinced?" Sean asked.

"Why don't you guys take this argument somewhere

else?" Brady suggested. Both men turned to look at him as if they'd forgotten he and Aine were there.

Shrugging, Sean said, "Good idea. Aine, nice to meet you."

"Thank you," she said, tearing her gaze from the images spilled across the gleaming oak table.

"Right," Mike said. "We'll be seeing you again soon, I know."

"I'm sure," she murmured, lost in the pen-and-ink sketches that were made more vivid by the bright splashes of color added sparingly, as if to draw the viewer's attention to the tiny details of the art itself.

When she and Brady were alone in the conference room, Aine laid her fingertip on the drawing of the great hall. She knew the room well, of course—it was a place the castle rented out for wedding receptions and the occasional corporate function. But this… There were medieval banners on the walls, tapestries that were colorful and in keeping with the era of the building itself. There were torches and candelabra and several long tables that would easily seat fifty each. The fireplace that hadn't been used in years looked as it should, trimmed with fresh stone and a wide mantel that displayed pewter jugs and goblets.

"What do you think?"

Truthfully, she didn't know what to think. Aine had been prepared to be appalled. Instead, she found herself intrigued by the artist's vision for the great hall and couldn't help wondering what else might surprise her. "This is—" she paused and lifted her gaze to his "—lovely."

A flicker of pleasure danced in his eyes and she responded to it.

"Your artist, Jenny, is it? She's very talented. The great hall looks as it might have when the castle was new and Lord Butler and his lady entertained."

"High praise from a woman afraid to see zombies and cobwebs all over her castle."

Hearing her own words tossed back at her only underscored her need to watch what she said in future. But for now, she lifted her chin and nodded in acceptance. "True enough, and I can admit when I'm wrong. Although I haven't seen all of your plans, have I?"

"So you're withholding praise until you're sure?"

"Seems wise, doesn't it?"

"It does," he agreed, then drew a few other images toward him. "So let me show you a few more."

For the next hour, Aine and Brady went over his plans for the castle. Though some of it sounded wonderful, there were other points she wasn't as fond of. "Gaming systems in all the bedrooms?" She shook her head. "That hardly seems in keeping with the castle's lineage."

He leaned back in his chair, reached for the cup of soda in front of him and took a drink. Then he leisurely polished off the last of his French fries. They'd had lunch sent in and Aine had hardly touched her club sandwich. How could she eat when her very future hung in the balance?

He had said he didn't want a yes man, someone to just agree with his pronouncements. But surely he would have a breaking point where he would resent having her argue with him over what was, to him and his partners, a very big deal.

"Even the people in the Middle Ages played games," he pointed out.

"Not on gigantic flat-screen televisions and built-in gaming systems."

Brady shook his head. "They would have if the tech had been around. And the televisions will be camouflaged in crafted cabinets to look period correct."

"That's something, I suppose," Aine said, knowing that she was being stubborn, but feeling as though she were fighting for the very life of the castle she loved.

He was covering her arguments one by one and he was doing it so easily she almost admired it. But she felt it was up to *her* to protect Castle Butler and the people who depended on it, so Aine would keep at her arguments in favor of tradition and history.

"And on the ground floor," she asked, "you want the dining room walls decorated with images from your game, yes?"

"That's the idea. It is Fate Castle after all."

"So the zombies and the wraiths will have their places there, as well."

"Yes."

She ground her teeth together. "You don't think people might be put off their food if they're surrounded by spirits of the dead looking over their shoulders?"

He frowned, tapped one finger against the table and said, "We can move the wall murals to the reception hall—"

Aine took a breath. "And what of the guests who *aren't* coming to be a part of role-playing?" she asked. "We've regular guests, you know, who return year after year and they're accustomed to a castle with dignity, tradition."

"You keep throwing around the word *tradition*, and yet, with all of that dignity, the castle is in desperate need of repair and almost broke."

She took a breath to fight him on that, but it was impossible to argue with an ugly truth. The castle she loved was in dire straits, and whether she liked it or not, Brady Finn was her only hope to save it. So many people depended on the castle and the guests who came to stay there that she couldn't risk alienating the man. Yet despite knowing all of that, she felt as though the castle itself was depending on her to preserve its heritage.

"I admit the castle needs some care and attention," she said, steeling herself to meet that clear, steady stare he'd fixed on her. "But I wonder if turning it into an amusement park is really the answer."

"Not an amusement park," he corrected. "No roller coasters, Ferris wheels or cotton-candy booths."

"Thank heaven for that, at least," she murmured.

"It's going to be a destination hotel," Brady told her and leaned forward, bracing his elbows on his knees. "People all over the world will want to come to Fate Castle and experience the game they love in real life."

"Fans, then."

"Sure, fans," he said, straightening abruptly and leaning back in his chair again. "But not only fans of the game. There'll be others. People who want a taste of a real medieval experience."

"Real?" she asked, tapping one finger on a drawing of a wraith with wild gray hair blowing in an unseen wind. "I've lived near the castle all my life and I've never seen anything like this haunting the grounds."

"Real with a twist," he amended, his lips twitching briefly.

That quick, thoughtless tiny half smile and her stomach did a quick dip and roll. She had to fight to keep her mind focused on their conversation. "And you believe there are enough fans of this game to turn the castle's finances around?"

He shrugged. "We sold one hundred million copies of Fate Castle."

Her mind boggled. The number was so huge it was impossible to believe. "So many?"

"And more selling all the time," he assured her.

She sighed, looked at the drawings spread out over the table and tried to mentally apply them to the castle she knew. It would be so different, she thought. Yet a voice in the back of her mind whispered, *It will survive*. If all went as Brady Finn suggested, the castle and the village it supported would continue. That was the most important thing, wasn't it?

"I suppose you're right, then, about fans coming to the castle. Though I worry about people like Mrs. Deery and her sister, Miss Baker."

He frowned. "Who are they?"

Aine sighed and brushed her hair back behind her ear. "Just two of our regular guests," she said. "They're sisters, in their eighties, and they've been coming to Castle Butler every year for the past twenty. They take a week together to catch up on each other's lives and to be coddled a little by the hotel staff."

"They can still come to the hotel," he said.

Aine glanced again at the drawing of the wraith. "Yes, they can and no doubt will. I just wonder what they'll make of the zombies…"

"It's not just the gaming aspects we're renovating at the castle," he said. "We'll be restoring the whole place. Making it safe again. The wiring's mostly shot. It's a wonder the place hasn't caught fire."

"Oh, it's not that bad," she argued, defending the place she loved.

"According to the building inspector we hired, it is," Brady said. "The plumbing will be redone, new roof, insulation—though the castle will look medieval, it won't feel like it."

Aine took a breath and held it to keep from saying anything else. He was right in that the building itself needed updating desperately. In winter, you could feel cold wind sliding between the stones. Under the window sashes it came through strong enough to make the drapes flutter.

"We're going to modernize the kitchens, install working furnaces and change out the worn or faded furniture. We'll be replacing woodwork that's rotted or ruined by water damage…"

All right, then, she thought, he was making her beloved castle sound like a tumbledown shack. "There've been storms over the years, of course, and—"

He held up one hand for silence and she was so surprised, she gave it to him.

"You don't have to defend every mantel and window sash in the place to me, Aine. I understand the castle's old…"

"Ancient," she corrected, prepared to defend anyway. "Historic."

"And we agree it needs work. I'm willing to have that work done."

"And change the heart of it," she said sadly.

"You're stubborn," he said. "I can appreciate that. So am I. The difference is, I'm the one who'll make the decisions here, Aine. You can either work with me or—"

She looked at him and read the truth in his cool blue eyes. Well, the implication there was clear enough. Get on board or get out. And since there wasn't a chance in hell she would willingly walk away from Castle Butler and all it entailed, she would have to bide her time, bite her tongue and choose very carefully the battles she was willing to wage.

With that thought in mind, she nodded and said, "Fine, then. If you must have the murals, why not put them in the great hall? You've said it's the place where your role players will gather. Wouldn't they be the ones to appreciate this kind of…art?"

His lips twitched again, and once more, she felt that quick jolt of something hot and…exciting zip through her like a lightning strike. *Ridiculous*, she told herself, ordering her hormones to go dormant.

She couldn't keep having these delicious little fantasy moments about her *boss*. Especially a boss who had made it abundantly clear that she was expendable. But it seemed that knowing she shouldn't had nothing to do with reality. Because just being in the same room with Brady Finn made her feel as if every inch of her skin was tingling.

Rather than answer her question immediately he said, "You have to admit that Jenny's sketches are good."

"They are," she said quickly, hoping to take her own mind off the path it continually wanted to wander. "For a game, they're wonderful. But as decoration in a hotel?"

"In *our* kind of hotel, they're perfect," Brady said firmly. "Though you have a point about the reception area. All right," he said, tapping a finger against the drawing of a howling banshee, "murals in the great hall."

"As easily as that?"

"I can compromise when the situation calls for it," he told her.

Nodding, she ticked off one win for herself on her

imaginary tote board. Naturally, Brady had more scores in this competition than she, but gaining this one compromise gave her hope for more. He wasn't implacable and that was good to know. Brady Finn would be difficult to deal with but not impossible.

"But," he added before complacency could settle in, "I will do things my way, Aine."

A warning and a challenge all in one, she told herself. No wonder the man fascinated her so.

The door opened after a soft perfunctory knock and a young woman stuck her head inside. "I'm sorry, Brady. But Peter's on the phone and he's insisting on speaking with you."

"That's fine, Sandy. Put him through." When the woman darted out again, Brady looked at Aine and said, "I have to take this call."

"Should I go?"

"No." He waved her down into her seat. "This won't take long and we're not finished."

Aine watched as he snatched up the receiver. The look on his face was hard, unforgiving, and she could have sworn ice chips swam in the blue of his eyes. She spared a moment of sympathy for Peter, whoever he was, as it looked as though he would regret interrupting Brady Finn.

"Peter?" Brady's voice was clipped, cool. "I'm not interested in more excuses."

A pause while the mysterious Peter babbled loudly enough for Aine to catch snatches of words. *Time—art—patience.*

"I've been more than patient, Peter. We all have been," Brady reminded the man, cutting his stream of excuses short. "That time is past. I told you what to expect if I didn't have those renderings by this afternoon."

More hurried, frantic talking from Peter in a voice that lifted into an outraged shout.

Brady frowned. "I'll have Sandy send you a check for the remainder of what we owe you."

Stunned silence filled the pause that followed that statement, and Aine could almost feel the unknown man's panic.

"Do yourself a favor and remember the confidentiality contract you signed with us, Peter. All drawings you've completed are our property, and if they leak to the competition…"

He smiled tightly and Aine noted the glint of satisfaction in his eyes. "Good. Glad to hear it. You're talented, Peter. If you can become focused, you'll have a solid career at some point. Just not here with us."

Aine felt a cold chill race along her spine and just managed to stifle the corresponding shudder. He had dismissed the unlamented Peter without a moment's hesitation. Would it be that easy for him to rid himself of *her*? That thought gave her pause and made her even more determined to watch her mouth and her temper.

When he hung up, Brady glanced at her and said, "Sorry about the interruption, but it couldn't be helped."

"Who's Peter?"

"An artist with more excuses than work," he said shortly. Maybe he caught the worry no doubt shining in her eyes because he added, "He was given more than one chance to come through. He failed."

"And so he's gone."

"Yeah," Brady said, gaze locked with hers. "Patience

only stretches so far. When it's business, you have to be able to make the hard choices."

But the thing was, Aine thought, firing Peter hadn't looked as if it was difficult for Brady at all. He'd ended the man's employment in a blink and now had moved on already to more pressing business. Aine felt the shaky bridge she stood upon tremble beneath her feet.

Four

Brady hadn't missed the wariness in her gaze as she'd listened to his conversation with Peter. Maybe he should have taken the call privately, but then again, it was probably best that she'd overheard him fire the man. She had to know that Brady was more than willing to dismiss any employee who couldn't do the work expected of them. He didn't enjoy that part of his job, but he wasn't reluctant to do what was necessary, either. He had nothing but respect for a hard worker and nothing but contempt for anyone who tried to slide out of their responsibilities by producing half-baked excuses.

Jenny Marshall would get her shot at being the lead artist on this project, and if she failed, he'd get rid of her, too. Brady and his partners worked hard, put everything they were into the job at hand, and damned if he'd accept anything less from the people around them.

"My brother, Robbie, would love this," she said as Brady steered her into the graphic-art division on the third floor of the old mansion.

There were desks, easels and plotting boards scattered around the big space. Computer terminals sat at every desk alongside jars holding pencils, pens, colored markers and reams of paper. Rock music pumped through the air, setting a beat that had a couple of the artists' chairs dancing, bobbing their heads and mouthing the words to the song. Every time Brady went into that room, he felt like the only earthling on Mars.

Someone had made popcorn in the bright red microwave, and the smell flavored every breath as he walked with Aine around the room.

"Some of our artists prefer doing all of the work on the computer, but most also enjoy the sensation of putting pen to paper, as well." He watched Aine sneaking peeks at works in progress. "It doesn't matter to me *how* they get the job done," Brady added, "as long as they do it well. And on schedule."

She slanted him a look. "Yes, I remember what happened to Peter."

Brady shrugged. "He had his chances and blew them all."

"You're not an easy man, are you?"

"*Nothing's* easy," he said, staring into the cool forest green eyes that had haunted him from the first moment he'd seen them. Then he took her arm and guided her around the room. As they walked, the buzz of conversations quieted. Brady knew that having the boss in the place would slow things down, but he wanted Aine to see all of Celtic Knot so she could appreciate exactly who it was she was working for.

He gave a meaningful glance to the people watching them and they all quickly got back to their work. Aine pulled away from him to take a closer look at a sketch one of the women was perfecting. When she came back to his side, Aine was smiling. "Oh, yes, Robbie would love all of this."

"Your brother?" he asked.

She glanced at him briefly. "Aye, I've told you he's mad for your games, but he's also an artist. A good one, too," she added with a quick, proud smile. "He'd be in heaven here, surrounded by talented people, drawing what he loves to draw."

"He wants to work on games?" Brady asked.

"It's his dream and one he's determined will come true," she said, pausing to look over the shoulder of a young man adding a wash of color to a sketch of a forest under moonlight.

"Lovely," she said, and the man turned to give her a wide grin.

Brady frowned, watching as Joe Dana turned on the charm and aimed it right at Aine. Annoyance—and something else—rose up inside and nearly choked him. He wasn't sure what the hell he was feeling, but he damn well knew he didn't like the way Joe was letting his gaze slide up and down Aine's curvy body.

"You've made the forest look alive," Aine told the man, giving him another smile.

"Thanks," Joe said, "but you haven't seen me add the werewolves yet."

"Werewolves?" She looked at the forest scene again. "But it's so pastoral, really, despite all the wild growth beneath the trees there. Adding monsters to it seems a shame."

"Monsters are what people like about games," Brady said, interrupting before Joe could speak again. At the sound of his boss's voice, the other man seemed to remember Brady's presence and shifted his focus from Aine to the sketch pad in front of him.

"We keep the soul of the art," Joe was saying as he deftly added a few dark strokes with a thick black marker, creating the shadowy outline of a werewolf, complete with dripping fangs. "'The Wolf of Clontarf Forest.' It'll be out sometime next year."

"Well, that's terrifying, isn't it?" Aine said to no one in particular. "And the forest looked so peaceful and dreamlike before…"

"That's one of the things our games are known for," Brady told her.

"Werewolves?"

Joe, the artist, laughed and said, "Not specifically. But the boss is right. We take something beautiful and make it dangerous. That's what makes it creepy. The danger lurking just beneath a placid surface."

Aine nodded and turned her gaze up to Brady's. In her eyes he saw the same danger lying beneath the serene surface she showed him. A different kind of jeopardy than some animated monster, Aine was like nothing he'd ever known before. There were fires within her, waiting to be stoked. Skin waiting to be caressed. And if he gave in to what he wanted, he'd be in even deeper trouble than if he stumbled across a werewolf.

"Clontarf?" she asked suddenly, her eyes narrowed suspiciously on him. "Are you making a game of the Battle of Clontarf?"

"We're using it as a backdrop, yeah. You've heard of it?"

Aine's eyes widened. "Every Irish child learns their history. The last high king of Ireland, Brian Boru, fought and died at Clontarf."

"He did," Brady said, impressed that she knew of it. He and the Ryan brothers did a lot of research into Irish history, not to mention the fact that the Ryans' parents were from Ireland and had raised their sons on the traditions and superstitions they remembered. At Celtic Knot, they preferred using actual historical figures and actions as stepping-off points to give their games another layer of reality. "I think you'll be impressed with the artwork of the actual battle scenes. Kids are going to love the gore factor of fighting with broadswords…"

"And you've turned it into a game?" She was horrified.

Joe Dana whistled low and long and hunched over his sketch pad. A couple of heads turned toward them, but Brady hardly noticed, so caught was he by the fury in Aine's gaze.

"King Brian defeated the Vikings, setting Ireland free, and died in the doing," she said, clearly outraged at having her country's history *borrowed* for entertainment.

"He did, and in our game, he'll do the same," Brady said coolly, taking her arm, ignoring the stiffness of her movements as he guided her through the room. "Only when Brian wins, it'll be because a legion of werewolves helped him. And if a player does well enough, he can be crowned the next high king of Ireland. Look at it this way," he said, "when people play this game, they'll be learning about your history. They'll play a game, fight for the Irish and learn all about King Brian Boru."

"Irish history doesn't include slavering werewolves." Aine shook her head and blew out a breath, obviously trying to relieve the rush of anger at seeing her country's heroes portrayed as part of a supernatural scenario. "I'm not sure if I should be impressed or appalled. Werewolves in Ireland?"

He shrugged and noticed the tension in her body was easing whether she realized it or not. "Why not? You guys believe in banshees, faeries, pookas… The list is long. Why not a werewolf?"

"True," she allowed, then cocked her head and looked up at him. "*You guys?* You still think you're not Irish."

Ignoring that, he frowned and guided her toward another artist's desk. "The storyboards for the games are laid out, checked for mistakes, and the scriptwriters work with the artists to lay in just enough dialogue to explain what's happening."

"So it's as you said, not just running and shooting?" Aine asked.

Her eyes were wide and interested, but he saw playfulness in those depths, too. "Much more than that. There are riddles, puzzles to solve. Mysteries to work out along the way."

"Ah, sure, the thinking man's video game, then," she said, humor evident in her tone.

Brady nodded. "Actually, that's exactly right."

He could see he'd surprised her with his response. But Brady thought her quip was right on the money. He and the Ryans prided themselves on the depth of the games they designed. While most people dismissed video entertainment as mindless, Celtic Knot Games had built a reputation for sophistication of story style and a narrative that, while rooted in fantasy, also boasted realism that drew a player into a role-playing world.

He took her arm and steered her out of the graphic design area and across the wide hall to a room on the other side of the house, where computers ruled.

"This is where our programmers take over," he said, then stepped back and allowed her to enter the room. He watched her as she wandered through the space, stopping at each desk where computer experts worked their keyboards. There were framed images taken from their games dotting the walls, and a sense of humming energy and creativity buzzed in the air. Music churned out, a wild rock beat giving the programmers a rhythm they matched with the rapid typing at the keyboards.

He could see where Aine might be fascinated by the programmers, who were, he noticed with a frown, pausing in their work to explain things to her. Normally, when you walked into this room, you were completely ignored. Like every other computer expert Brady had ever met, the guys in here didn't see anything beyond what was on their screens. Hell, Brady himself had been in here when he'd had to shout to get their attention—but every man in the room had suddenly become focused on Aine Donovan. He couldn't blame them, but damned if he enjoyed watching the scene play out in front of him.

She laughed at something one of them said and Brady's insides fisted at the sound. She let her head fall back, and all that amazing hair of hers seemed to flow down her back like a molten river. She reached out and laid one hand on a programmer's shoulder as she leaned in to see what he wanted to show her on the screen, and Brady's frown deepened. Jealous of a friendly touch? No, he assured himself. The idea was ridiculous. But for completely unrelated reasons, he ended the visit to the programming room and steered Aine back into the hall.

"It's all very impressive," she said, "though I'll admit I don't understand half of what it is you do here."

"That's all right," he said, guiding her down the stairs to the main hall. "I wouldn't know how to manage a castle, would I?"

She sent him a long look. "I've a feeling that you'd find a way to excel at it."

"I would," he agreed, leading her along the hall and toward the French doors that led to the patio and backyard. "But since you're already an expert, I don't need to be."

She stepped outside and walked into a patch of sunlight that dappled through the surrounding elms. A soft ocean breeze rustled the leaves and lifted her hair from her shoulders. Turning to face him, she said, "And as your manager, I'll be in charge of seeing the changes made to the castle."

"That's right."

"And you'll give me a list, I suppose."

"More than that," he said and gestured to a table and chairs. They took seats beside each other and Brady said, "Over the next three weeks, you and I will be working on the plans for the castle—"

"Three weeks?"

Her surprise sounded in her voice even if he hadn't seen it in her eyes. Brady paid no attention and continued, "I'll want your input on some of the changes to the bedrooms, the furnishings, the setup to the new kitchens. There we want the medieval look and feel but naturally all modern appliances…"

"I'm sorry," she interrupted. "Did you say three weeks?"

"Yeah." He looked at her. "Is that a problem?"

"I never thought I'd be here that long."

Brady watched her and could almost see the wheels of her brain turning. She chewed at her bottom lip, and the action tugged at something inside him. Her face was an open book, he thought. There was no artifice there, no poker face. She obviously wasn't as used to schooling her features as he was.

But then, he'd spent a lifetime hiding what he was feeling from the rest of the world.

And over the years that had become easier because Brady had simply avoided feeling anything at all. Friendship was one thing. He couldn't stop caring for the Ryan brothers because they were the only family he'd ever known. Cutting them out of his life would be impossible even if he wanted to. It hadn't been easy, lowering his defenses enough to let them in, but Mike and Sean had simply refused to be shut out of Brady's life. They'd steamrolled over his objections and had drawn him into a circle of friendship he'd never known before them.

They were the only people who saw Brady's laughter or anger or fears. They were the only people he trusted that much. And he had no intention of risking anyone else getting that close. Especially a woman who worked for him.

Didn't mean he couldn't enjoy the rush of desire that came out of nowhere to knock his legs out from under him.

"Three weeks," she repeated, more to herself than to him.

"Is there a problem?" He heard the stiffness in his own voice and didn't bother to soften it. She worked for Celtic Knot, whether she was in Ireland or America.

She responded to his tone and he watched as she squared her shoulders and lifted her chin. Why those subtle movements would affect him as much as a more sensual move would have was beyond him.

"Three weeks is a long time when you're not prepared for it," she said, then she became thoughtful. "I can call home, let the staff know I won't be about, and then call my mother…"

Now she surprised him. "Your mother?"

"She'd worry otherwise, wouldn't she?"

"I wouldn't know," Brady said simply. How the hell would he know what mothers were like? His own had dropped him off at Child Services when he was six years old, with the promise to come back by the end of the week. He'd never seen her again. As for the Ryan brothers, whenever they went home to visit with their folks, Brady stayed away. He'd gone with them once, during college. And though their parents had made every effort, Brady had spent that incredibly long weekend too uncomfortable to accept their open hospitality. He had no idea how to deal with the threads of family and he told himself it was too damn late now to try to understand it. Not that he wanted to.

Aine looked at him in confusion, but that expression quickly faded. "I'm happy to stay, of course," she said a little too tightly to be believable. "I'll help in any way I can, obviously."

"Good." He nodded shortly and refused to acknowledge the fact that the next three weeks with Aine Donovan were going to be a test of the self-control he'd always prided himself on. Hell, even sitting here beside her in the sunlight was making him burn. Watching her eyes narrow on him kindled those slow-moving flames inside him until his skin buzzed with expectation. She was unexpected, but damned if he could regret having her drop into his lap—so to speak.

Maybe he would regret it later. But for right now, that quickening fire was all he could think about.

For the next week, Aine felt as if she was living in a tornado—the Brady Finn Tornado. It seemed he was tireless. They roamed through countless antiques stores—and Brady kept insisting that old furniture was the same, whether European or American. She'd fought him on several tables, chairs and even a bed or two, and to give the man his due, he was willing to be nudged away from his first decision when offered a better choice. But he was monopolizing her time. They were together every day and talked of what still needed to be done over dinner.

And every day it became just a little bit harder to ignore the heat she felt just being around him.

Ridiculous, and she knew it, to feel this way, but it appeared she had no control over her body's reaction to a man she had no business getting dizzy over. He was autocratic, opinionated, and he tended to speak to her as if he were expecting her to pull a steno tablet from her bag and start taking notes.

If anything, she should be infuriated at his domineering attitude. Yes, he was her employer, but he wasn't the Prince of Wales, was he? And even if he were, Aine admitted, an Irishwoman wouldn't be bowing down to him.

But instead of this very rational reaction to being ordered about on a daily basis, Aine spent entirely too much time watching his mouth as he spoke, wondering what his lips would feel like. Taste like. And it wasn't as if she could escape these thoughts when she slept, because her dreams were full of him, as well.

Because, she acknowledged, bossy and controlling wasn't all there was to the man. She'd also seen him stop and hold a door for a woman burdened down with bags of groceries. Whenever they went walking he never failed to drop a bill or two into the open cases of street musicians or to hand money to a homeless man holding a cardboard sign. He was a confusing mixture of rough and kind, of sharp and soft, and he fascinated her more with every passing day.

"I think that takes care of today's business," Brady said, snapping Aine's attention back to him.

The sea wind ruffled his dark hair like fingers running through it and Aine folded her own fingers into her palm to avoid the urge to do it herself. He pulled off dark glasses and laid them on the table in front of him. Lunch at this sidewalk café in Newport Beach had become something of a habit over the past week. Here was where they sat, went over his plans and purchases made for the castle.

"Really? No more looking for just the right linens today, then?"

He slanted her a sardonic look. "You don't want to shop? I never thought I'd hear that particular statement from a woman."

"Allow me to be the first," Aine said, picking up her tea and taking a sip. She winced slightly at the taste and idly wished for a *real* cup of tea. "'Tis fair, I think, to say that my shopping quota has been met for the year, at least."

"Tired of looking at towels, huh?"

"You aren't?"

"I couldn't be more bored," he admitted and picked up his coffee for a long drink. "But it's important that we have everything just as it should be at this new hotel. Even down to the towels."

While she could admire his attention to detail, it surprised her that the owner of a hotel was taking such personal responsibility for every aspect of his business. "I agree," she said, tipping her head to one side to watch him. "It's only that the previous owner never bothered with such minutiae so I'm a bit surprised."

He set his coffee cup down. "But the previous owner ended up losing his hotel to me, didn't he?"

"True."

"I don't lose," he said shortly.

She was willing to bet that Brady Finn had never lost anything important to him. What must it be like, she wondered, to live a life so ruthlessly organized? So completely in your control? Aine smiled to herself at the very idea of being so sure of yourself that you could reorder the world around you to suit your needs. She knew all too well that the wealthy had no idea how the real world lived, and Brady's arrogance only seemed to highlight that opinion. He expected things to go his way, so they did. If he met an obstacle, it was probably his nature to roll right over it. He wouldn't be stopped. Wouldn't be changed. Wouldn't be ignored.

And God help her, she found all of that fascinating. She shouldn't, Aine knew. But how could she ignore what it was that happened to her when he was near—or on those rare occasions when he actually touched her? A casual brush of his hand against hers. His hand at the small of her back when he guided her through one of the innumerable shops they'd been through in the past several days? The flash of pride she felt when he turned and asked her opinion on something. The look in his eyes when he would stop suddenly and stare at her as if she'd simply dropped from the sky.

All of this and more was what fed the dreams that kept her restless every night and woke her feeling on edge, as though she was standing on a precipice and needed only the slightest push to tumble over. It was pointless to have these feelings, to indulge in dreams that would lead nowhere, she knew. The chasm separating them was too wide, and deep. A woman from a small rural village in Ireland had nothing in common with a multimillionaire.

"Is there a problem?"

His voice, deep, low and somehow intimate, tore her from her thoughts. "I'm sorry, what was that?"

"A problem?" he asked. "You went quiet, and the look on your face tells me you're trying to think your way out of something."

Wasn't it an annoying thing, she thought, to not have your thoughts remain your own? "So easy to read, am I?"

One corner of his mouth lifted briefly. "Poker? Not your game."

"Humiliating, but true enough," she said on a sigh. Heaven knew he wasn't the first person to see what she was thinking by studying her expression. Hopefully, though, he wouldn't be able to suss out exactly what it was she felt when he was close. Her humiliation then would know no bounds. "But no, there's no problem. I'm only thinking about home, wondering what's happening while I'm gone."

"You live with your mother and brother, don't you?"

She looked at him and saw speculation in his eyes. "Yes, and you're wondering why at my age I would be."

He nodded and waited for whatever she had to say next.

Sighing a bit, Aine said, "The truth is, I moved out

when I was twenty. Took a flat in the village and loved having my own space." She smiled, remembering. "I love my family, but—"

"I get it," he said companionably.

Her smile widened, then slipped away. "But then, five years ago, my father died."

"Sorry."

He looked uncomfortable, as most people did when faced with something they couldn't change or help with.

"Thank you." Aine smiled at him again, letting him know she was fine. She still missed her father, but the worst of the pain had faded over the years. She could talk about him now, think about him, without a crushing ache settling into her heart. "He was a fisherman and there was a ferocious storm one night. He never came home." She frowned then, remembering how their family had changed so suddenly. "My mother was wrecked. Shattered without him, as he was the love of her life. They'd been together so long and had been true partners in everything. Without him, she was lost and didn't want to be found. So I moved back home to help her care for Robbie, who was only twelve at the time and just as lost as Mum."

"Must have been hard."

She saw a glimmer of understanding in his eyes and responded to it. "It was, for some time. But things are better now and Mum is not so sad as before."

"So you put your life on hold for your family."

She shrugged. "'Tis what you do for those you love."

He frowned a bit at that, and Aine wondered about it. Did he not understand after all? Had he no one in his life to matter so much? Her heart twisted at that thought.

"You miss it?"

"Ireland, you mean?" Surprised at the question, she said, "'Tis natural, isn't it? It's home after all."

"Right." He nodded, set his coffee aside and said, "Tell me about it."

"About Ireland?"

That half smile appeared again and vanished in a blink. "Not all of it, just your part. The village. The castle."

All around them, people laughed and talked. Waiters moved through the cluster of tables with the easy rhythm of long practice. The hum of traffic from the street became a drone of sound that mimicked the ocean just half a block away. Sunlight slanted through a bank of white clouds and glinted off the glass-topped tables.

As lovely as it was, the scene around her was a lifetime and more from what Aine knew and loved. She took a breath, smiled as she drew up the familiar images in her mind and started talking.

"The village is small but has everything we need in it. If you're wanting more of a shopping experience, Galway city is but an hour's drive." Her voice softened as she described the country that seemed so very far away. "As I've always lived there, I might be a bit biased, but it's a lovely village and the people are warm and friendly. The roads are narrow, lined with thick hedgerows of gorse and fuchsia—"

He laughed shortly. "Those are plants?"

She grinned. "Yes, fine, heavy hedges that bloom with yellow and red flowers in spring and early summer. You drive down roads so narrow that sometimes it's a wonder two cars could pass each other. Farms abound, with their stone walls and grazing cows and sheep. There are ruins, of course," she said, bracing her forearms on the warm tabletop. "Conical towers and the remains of castles long fallen stand near stone dances where, if you listen closely enough, you can hear the echoes of voices from the past."

Her gaze caught his and she stared into those deep, guarded eyes as she said softly, "The sky is so blue in Ireland you could weep for it. And when the clouds roll in from the Atlantic, they carry with them either fine, soft rain or storms vicious enough to moan through the stones of the castle until it sounds as if souls are screaming."

A moment of silence ticked past before Brady spoke and shattered the spell she'd woven for herself.

"Souls screaming," he repeated thoughtfully. "That'll go well with the guests at Fate Castle."

"That's what you heard? Something to help with your business?" she asked, wondering if he ever thought of anything else.

"It's not all I heard," he said. "But it's my main interest. It's why you're here, isn't it?" he asked with a shrug. "If not for my buying the castle, you'd still be in Ireland trying to think of a way to save the hotel you manage."

So he'd heard nothing of the magic of Ireland in her description. Only the barest facts as it concerned his latest business. "You've a way of boiling things down to their center, don't you?"

"No point in pretending otherwise, is there?"

"I suppose not," she said, and knew he was probably reading her expression again. This time what he would see was exasperation, and she was comfortable with that. She might be determined to keep her temper, but the fact that the man could so easily dismiss a hotel that had been in operation for decades—never mind the centuries-old castle itself—was still annoying.

He laughed, and the sound was so surprising she forgot her momentary irritation. "What's funny?"

"You. You're insulted on behalf of your castle."

"As you've continually pointed out, 'tis not mine but *your* castle," she said more stiffly than she'd wanted.

"And yet..." He tipped his head to one side and asked, "So in all the descriptions of your Ireland, I didn't hear any mention of a man. No one there for you to particularly miss?"

Now it was Aine's turn to frown as she realized she was the one doing all the sharing and talking here and he was as much a mystery to her today as he had been in the beginning. But maybe, she thought, by opening up herself, she would find it easier to pry information from him.

"No," she said at last, "there's no one now."

"Now?"

"There was," she told him. "I was engaged once. Brian Feeny." She paused and realized that she could remember him now, talk about him now and not feel even the slightest echo of pain or regret. "He's an accountant living in Dublin. I heard he's married and happy."

"Why'd you break up?"

"Why's that your business?"

"It isn't," he said simply.

She laughed shortly. "Fine, then. 'Twas nothing dramatic. It was only that my family needed me and Brian couldn't understand how I would put them before him. Us."

"Most men probably wouldn't," he told her.

"Would you?"

"I know that if the Ryan brothers needed me, I'd be there no matter what anyone else needed from me." He shrugged negligently. "Does that answer the question?"

"Aye," she said, "it does." She took a breath and admitted, "When it ended, I wasn't heartbroken or devastated or even really disappointed. And I knew then that I hadn't really loved him. Not enough."

She'd *wanted* to love Brian, but she simply hadn't had it in her. And maybe she never would know the kind of love her parents had had. But then, loving that deeply, that completely—that carried its own risks, didn't it? She remembered clearly how broken her mother had been at the loss of her love, and Aine had to wonder if the pain of it was worth the loving.

"Or maybe it wasn't you at all, and it was just this Brian being a jackass," Brady said.

Her gaze snapped to his and a slow smile curved her mouth. She'd never really considered it from that angle.

"That's enough depth for today, I think. How about a walk?" He stood up and held out one hand to her.

Surprise flickered through her again. Aine looked from his eyes to his extended hand and back again. She hesitated only a moment or two before laying her hand in his. Exasperation aside, the man was not only her employer but was currently beguiling her. When her hand met his, heat dazzled her and she fought with everything she had to keep him from seeing her reaction to the connection between them. "I'd like that. I feel as if I've been indoors for days."

"We'll walk to the pier, then," he said, folding his fingers around her hand and tugging her along beside him. "You can watch the Pacific and think of the Atlantic."

Five

Aine knew she'd be hard-pressed to think of anything but him as long as he was beside her, but she was eager for the cold sea wind. Maybe it would help douse the fire inside her.

For a woman accustomed to the quiet of a rural Irish village, the constant pound of noise—from traffic and hundreds of people—was distracting. Aine thought she'd become accustomed to the bustle and rush in the past week or more, but when she and Brady walked to the end of the pier, she sighed in relief and smiled to herself. Here there was only the rush of the waves to the beach, the call of seabirds and the creak of the pier itself as it rocked in the water. She took a deep breath of the ocean air and tipped her face back to the sky, letting the sunlight wash over her skin.

"I think this is the first time I've seen you relaxed since you got here," Brady said.

"It's the sea," she answered, sliding a look at him. "The waves here are calmer, softer than at home, where the water can rage, but the sound of it, like a heartbeat, 'tis soothing after all the noise of the main street. I think if I had so many people about me all of the time, I might lose my mind."

"And I think having nothing but quiet around me all the time would do the same."

Another point to show how ill matched they were, Aine thought, as if she had needed more. "Is that why you've not come to Ireland to see your castle in person?"

"Not really," he said, tucking both hands into his pockets. He turned his face into the wind. "There's no need for me to be there with you on scene to report."

"What about the curiosity factor, then?" she asked, plucking her wind-blown hair from her eyes.

He glanced at her. "There isn't one," he said. "Not about this."

Both of her eyebrows flew up. "You'd spend millions on a castle, invest even more in making it into what you've imagined and have no desire to see it yourself?"

"If there's a problem you can't handle, I'll consider it." He cocked his head to one side. "*Is* there a problem you can't handle?"

"I've not found one yet," she said.

"There you go, then. I've got the right manager."

"I like to think so." Yet his attitude still puzzled her. How was it a man could be so involved in a project the size of this one and have no interest in being a part of it beyond writing checks? Then she remembered how he'd denied being Irish in spite of the name that gave away his heritage, and Aine wondered if it was the castle he was avoiding or Ireland itself. The mystery of that question only made her wonder more about Brady Finn.

"I've been wondering…"

"Never good when a woman says that," he mused.

A wry smile touched her mouth briefly. "You said once that the only thing Irish about you is your name."

He stiffened and a rigid look came over his face. "Yeah."

"What did you mean?"

She thought for a moment he wasn't going to answer her at all. His gaze shifted from her eyes to the wide sweep of sea spilling out before them. Aine kept quiet, waiting, hoping that because she had opened up about her own past he would bend and give her a glimpse of the man inside.

"I mean," he finally said, "I didn't grow up with the legends of Ireland like you. Or with Irish music and pride of heritage like the Ryans." His big hands curled over the top bar of the pier railing and he leaned into the wind as it blew his thick dark hair back from his face. "I grew up—" He bit the words off before he could say more. "Doesn't matter. A name's just a name. The Irish thing is as foreign to me as America is to you, I imagine." He was scowling as if he'd said more than he wanted to, even though it was pitifully little as far as Aine was concerned.

"Your family wasn't interested in their roots? Where they came from?" she asked, more curious than ever now, though she could see clearly he'd no wish to speak of his past.

"I didn't have a family," he said shortly, his tone demanding an end to the conversation.

He meant it, that was plain. She couldn't imagine it, having no one to call your own. To not have the solid base of a family to stand upon and build a life. Her heart hurt for him, even though she knew he wouldn't want it to. A proud man he was, and even admitting to that small piece of his past would have torn at him. So she let it go. For now.

"And yet now you own a castle in Ireland," she said softly.

He shot her a look. "It doesn't mean anything."

Or, she thought, he didn't *want* it to mean anything.

"I've noticed a few things about you myself the past several days." He turned to face her, and with the wide sweep of ocean behind him, he could have been a pirate, with his dark good looks and sharp cobalt eyes. The collar of his black bomber jacket was turned up against the wind and his hair blew around his face like a dark halo.

God help her, he took her breath away.

"What is that?" she asked finally, when she knew she could speak without her voice breaking.

"You're as focused as I am," he said, "as determined to get things right. Though it makes you crazy, you're protecting your castle by changing what you think of as the heart of it."

She shifted, still uncomfortable at being read so easily. Why was it, she wondered, that he could see so clearly into her when who he was remained a mystery to her?

"Its heart will still be there," she assured him, "as will its soul. I'll make sure of it. But no, I'm not fighting you on most of it because what would be the point? I work for you. You own the castle."

"And if I didn't?"

"What?" She looked up at him. The sun was positioned right behind him, gilding the outline of his body. His eyes were shadowed, and she wasn't sure if that was good or bad. She couldn't try to figure out what he might be thinking if she couldn't see his eyes—but on the other hand, not being able to look into those deep blue eyes might help her keep from making a fool of herself.

"If I didn't own the castle—" He moved in closer to her, and Aine's heart galloped in her chest. Her mouth was dry, her stomach twisting into knots. Anxious, Aine took a breath and held it.

She could feel the heat of him reaching out to her. They were alone here at the end of the pier, with only the sigh of the ocean waves as they surged toward shore. Sunlight streamed from a sky studded with thick white clouds, and the cool sea breeze wrapped itself around the two of them, as if trying to draw them closer. Aine swallowed hard and forced herself to stand her ground, though it might have been safer all around if she'd taken a step back.

"If you didn't own the castle, I wouldn't be here at all, would I?"

He nodded. "Then, it's good I do own it, isn't it?"

"I suppose." Oh, at the moment, she thought it was very good indeed that he'd brought her here and that they had wandered to this spot of privacy in the middle of the city.

"And this thing between us?" His voice dropped until it became a rush of sound as deep as the ocean. "Do you think that's good, too?"

She flushed. She felt it; she only hoped he couldn't see it. How humiliating to be a woman near thirty and feel heat flood her cheeks. But it wasn't voluntary, was it? Wasn't her fault that he triggered something inside her that made her every reaction to him twice as fast and hot as anything she'd ever known. And he asked if she was glad of the thing burning between them? Whether she was or not, it was there and as each day passed, more difficult to ignore. But that didn't mean she had to speak of it with him.

"I don't know what you mean—"

"Don't pretend," he said, cutting her off before she could tell a hopeless lie. "We both feel it. Have from the first." He laid his hand over hers where it rested on the top bar of the pier railing.

His touch set off sparks and flames that hissed and burned inside her until it felt as if her skin was bubbling with the intensity. Blast him for touching her, for making it impossible to ignore what she felt around him or to hide those feelings from him.

"All right, then, yes," she said and tugged her hand free. "There's something…"

"We've been together every day for more than a week, and it's time we talked about this."

Aine laughed shortly and shook her head. "Talk about it? To what end?" she asked. "We're both of us adults. Just because we feel a thing doesn't mean we'll act on it."

"And we won't," he said. "That's what I wanted to talk about. It would be a mistake to do anything about this. I'm your boss."

"I know that," Aine said, feeling the first flare of anger erupt. "'Tisn't necessary for you to warn me away from you or to tell me I've to keep my hormones in check around you. I'm not planning to have my wicked way with you, Brady Finn. Your honor is safe with me."

He shook his head. "You keep surprising me, Aine."

"Well, I'll say the same to you," she answered, folding her arms across her chest and taking that one all-important step backward. "This is the first conversation of the type I've ever had."

"Me, too," he said. "Usually, when I want a woman, I just go after her."

She cocked her head and gave him a narrowed look. "And she falls gratefully into your manly arms?"

He laughed, and the transformation his face went under was enough to take her breath away. A handsome man when frowning, he was staggering when he smiled.

"Most of the time, yeah."

"It's disappointed I am in my gender," Aine said, then reached up and pushed her windblown hair out of her eyes. "As for being one of the few who've managed to resist your *charms*, I'm doubly glad to take a stand for myself as I'd have no interest in being part of a crowd anyway."

"You wouldn't be," he said and his voice lost all trace of amusement. "You're one of a kind, Aine. I've never met anyone quite like you."

"Thanks for that," she said, then added, "and at the risk of inflating an ego too many women before me have stroked, I'll say the same of you." She tipped her head back to meet the shadowed eyes she *felt* watching her with tightly restrained hunger.

He gave her a nod. "Then, it's good we're not doing this."

"Absolutely. 'Tis the sensible solution."

"This is business," Brady said. "Sex would just confuse the situation."

And, oh, she thought she might really love to be confused by this man. But clearly, he was more interested in backing away from her as quickly as he could. "You're right again."

He moved in closer. "It's good we talked about it. Cleared the air. Got things settled."

"It is." She leaned toward him. "I'm sure we'll both be better off now and able to focus on our shared task."

"Concentration is good."

"A laudable talent."

Nodding, gaze locked with hers, he whispered, "We're not going to be sensible, are we?"

"Not at the moment, no," she said.

Then he kissed her.

The first touch of his mouth to hers turned Brady's world upside down. He'd expected heat, the flash of desire, the hunger that had been building in him for the past week. What he hadn't expected was the compulsion to devour. The frantic need to pull her closer, tighter to him, to feel her body bend to his. Her arms circled his neck; her fingers threaded through his hair, nails scraping along his scalp.

Her mouth opened under his, and the first taste of her staggered him until he was forced to lock his knees to keep from simply sagging to the ground beneath the onslaught of sensations. No woman had ever done this to him before. Hell, he hadn't known he *could* feel like this. Sex was easy. Desire was enjoyable, naturally. But this fire was unlike anything else he'd ever experienced. He fisted his hands at the small of her back and held her with arms of steel.

One taste awakened the need for more, and a wild voice in his mind whispered a taste would never be enough. He wanted to drown in her, feel her legs wrap around his hips and hold his body deeply within hers. Even as those thoughts beat at his brain, he fought against them. Wanting her was okay. *Needing* was something else.

She moaned, and the soft sound whispered into his mind, bringing him to his senses before he could lose his grip on the last tattered threads of his self-control. Hell, they were locked together in broad daylight where anyone could walk up and get an eyeful. It cost him, but he tore his mouth free, then rested his forehead against hers while he caught his breath and tried to find his way back to sanity. It wasn't easy.

What the hell was wrong with her ex-fiancé? What kind of man made the decision to marry a woman like Aine, then gave her up? Brady wasn't looking for forever, but he didn't want to let her go, either.

"Well, then," she murmured, the Irish in her voice singing as she, too, fought for air, "that was an unexpected feast."

He laughed shortly. "It was." Lifting his head, he looked down at her, saw her green eyes shining, glittering, and steeled himself against giving in to the impulse to grab her and taste her again. Give in once and he might never let her go, and that was unacceptable.

"And," he said firmly, as much to himself as to her, "now that we've got that out of our systems, working together will go much more smoothly."

She blew out a breath, then lifted both hands to scoop them through her hair. After a moment, she nodded. "So then, you kissed me, half devoured me, for the sake of the work?"

At the word *devoured*, his body tightened, but he said only, "Yes. We both felt the tension all week. I thought it would be a good idea to just give in and get it out of the way. Now the urge's been satisfied."

Not nearly, his brain screamed. In fact, if he had her over, under, around him for weeks, Brady doubted his hunger for her would be quenched.

"I see." She nodded, turned her face into the wind and stared out to sea for a long moment before speaking. "Then, I'll thank you for being so brave as to throw yourself on a live grenade such as myself—for the good of the work."

Brady frowned. Figured she'd take this the wrong way. Had she even *once* reacted to something the way he thought she would? It wasn't as if he'd sacrificed himself by kissing her—it was only that he didn't want her to get the wrong idea about that kiss. "I didn't say that."

"Aye, you did." She whipped her gaze back to his. Her green eyes flashed, and damned if he didn't want her even more than he had before that kiss. "Why, it was practically *saintly* how you took on the chore of teaching me a lesson. You kissed me for my own good. To make sure I can work with you and stay focused on my job rather than wasting time with idle daydreams of *you*."

With every word she spoke, Brady felt like more of an ass. Which he didn't appreciate. "I didn't say that, either," he ground out.

"Oh, what a trial it must be for you," she continued, tipping her head back to glare at him. "Being so handsome and rich and such a *magnet* for women. Why, you should think about hiring a bodyguard to protect you from those you haven't had time to teach how to control themselves."

"For—" Brady shoved one hand through his hair and muttered, "You're putting words in my mouth, Aine."

"You might as well have said them yourself."

"No. I say exactly what I mean," Brady told her and

shot a quick glare at some tourist who was wandering too close to them. The man immediately turned and walked the other way. Brady refocused on Aine. "I don't need you guessing what I might have meant. You won't have to. I'll tell you exactly what I'm thinking."

"As you have," she said, folding both arms across her chest and then tapping her fingertips against her upper arms. "Well, you'll be happy to know I agree with you. It was a lovely kiss, I'm sure, but you needn't worry I'll swoon into your arms demanding another."

Gritting his teeth, Brady's eyes rolled back briefly. "Swoon?"

"Or throw myself at your feet," she continued as if he hadn't spoken. "As I said, it was a lovely kiss, but it wasn't enough to drive me into a rage of frustrated lust. I'm here to do a job, and I intend to do it and then go home. You're completely safe from my wiles." She paused only long enough to take a breath, then added, "I've been kissed before and managed to hold on to my sanity."

He barked out a sharp laugh.

"'Tisn't funny," she snapped.

Yeah, it was. He knew she was lying because he'd felt her reaction to that kiss. Didn't matter how she tried to bluff her way out of it. She'd been as rocked by it as he was, and hearing her lie about it now made him smile. The woman kept him guessing all the time. Strange how much he was beginning to like it. "Damn. You've got a mouth on you, I'll give you that."

She flushed a bit at that. "What it is about you that makes my temper boil over, I don't know. But I'll not apologize for what I've said, even if you fire me for it."

"Who said anything about firing you?"

"No one, as of yet. Mind, I won't be kissing you again,

Brady Finn, so if it's all the same to you, keep your own mouth to yourself in the future."

"That's the plan," he said, though it wouldn't be easy. But then what the hell else in his life had *ever* been easy?

"Then, we've an agreement on this." While he watched, she turned and started walking away from him.

For a long moment, Brady admired the view. Coming or going, Aine Donovan was a feast for any man's eyes. But, he reminded himself sternly as his gaze dropped to the curve of her behind, he wasn't looking for a feast.

His hands curled into fists as he started after her. The sun was just dipping toward the ocean, the light fading into a soft twilight. In the last rays of the sun, her dark red hair looked alight with fire. She was more than he'd expected. More than he wanted. The only answer, he thought as he caught up to her and took hold of her upper arm in a firm grip that had her turning her green eyes to his, was to finish their business and get her back to Ireland as quickly as possible.

She tried to tug free of his grip, but Brady kept hold of her.

"Let go of me," Aine said, her eyes flashing.

"Trust me, I'll be doing that just as soon as I can," Brady assured her, steering her down the pier and back to the crowds along Pacific Coast Highway.

"How are things at home, Mum?" Aine paced the hotel suite that felt, at the moment, like a lavishly decorated cage. She was tense, on edge, and because she couldn't stop thinking about that kiss she'd shared with Brady just a few hours ago, it was only getting worse. Every cell in her body felt as if it were on fire. Her skin was buzzing and her concentration was simply shot.

She'd always prided herself on her ability to compartmentalize things in her life. But now her personal life was sliding into her business life, and she didn't know how to stop it. Or worse, even if she *wanted* to stop it. Then there was the problem of forever losing her temper with the man who could fire her with a word. Oh, God help her, life would be so much easier if only she was home again.

"Oh, it's been noisy as ten drums about here lately," Molly Donovan said. "There's lorries coming and going from the castle dozens of times a day. Some American men arrived today, construction people they say they are, only waiting for everything to be readied before they begin fixing the castle."

"American crews?" Aine asked, interrupting her mother before the woman could get on such a roll she wouldn't be stopped. "Are there no local men working there?"

"Not so far, but they've not started as yet. Just carting in half of Ireland in the way of rocks and lumber and what have you." Her mother clucked her tongue and added, "Although Danny Leary is down to the pub telling all who'll listen that it should be Irish workmen bringing our own castle back to life."

Aine sighed, and rested her forehead against the cold glass of the French doors. Danny Leary ran the best construction crews in County Mayo, and if he was unhappy with the work situation, that meant word of this was spreading throughout the county. People wouldn't be pleased. Sure, the idea of Castle Butler being renovated was a good one, but if the people at home didn't feel a part of it, how could they support it? And if those in the village wanted to, they could make the work very hard indeed. They could block roads—*accidentally*, of course—and slow down deliveries. All manner of things could go wrong. This could end up being a huge mess, all because Brady Finn wouldn't listen when she'd told him to hire local crews.

"I'm sure it'll all be fine," her mother was saying. "As soon as you tell your Mr. Finn that he'd do better to use Irish hands on the job."

"I've told him, Mum," Aine admitted on another sigh, remembering their conversation about just this not long after she'd arrived. "'Tis clear now he wasn't listening."

"And since when is it that you couldn't make yourself heard, Aine Donovan?" Molly's voice went as firm as steel and Aine winced as she recognized the no-nonsense tone. "You've a place there. And a voice. Your Mr. Finn—"

"He's not *my* anything, Mum," Aine interrupted, ignoring the stir of something inside her, "except my employer, who could fire me at a whim."

"And why would he do that?" her mother countered. "Didn't he fly you to California like a queen on her own plane? Hasn't he kept you there for more than a week already to listen to your ideas?"

"Yes, but—"

"Hasn't he told you more than once that he values an honest opinion and not simply the mindless nattering of a yes man?"

"He has, but—"

"Let me ask you this," Molly continued.

Ask away, Aine thought, and wondered if her mother would let her get a word in to answer whatever question was coming.

"Are you good at your job, Aine?"

"Of course I am." That wasn't in question.

"Do you know what's best for the castle and the village?"

"I do." Aine swallowed her impatience, as it wouldn't do her a bit of good when dealing with her mother. Besides, she thought, Molly was right in all she was saying, but that didn't mean Aine could repeat any of it to Brady. Yes, he'd said he wanted to hear her opinions, but there was a coolness to him, something that kept everyone around him at a distance.

Of course, her mind whispered, there'd been no distance between them at all when he'd kissed her out on the pier, with the waves crashing below and the wind swimming around them in a cold embrace. No, he hadn't held back then, and neither had she, though she nearly cringed to admit that. Though he'd done a quick step away when the kiss ended and had managed to insult her all at the same time.

He was her boss. With the power to dismiss her from the job she loved. He was a wealthy man with all the expectations of the rich, no doubt. If he wanted something, he took it, and be damned to consequences. Well, she was one who had to think of what might be. And kissing Brady Finn again would be another foolish step along a road that could only lead her to regret.

"Then, Aine," her mother said, drawing her attention back to the matter at hand, "you must speak up. You must do what you can for all of our sakes. The man's a businessman. He'll surely see the right of it when you lay it out for him plainly." Then she half covered the phone receiver and said, "Robbie, your sister's in no mind to answer questions from you about the silly games."

Aine couldn't help but smile. Her younger brother was fascinated by computer games, and Celtic Knot's in particular. If he'd had his way, Robbie would have been on the plane with her to visit the offices of his favorite gaming company.

Her mother sighed. "Robbie says to ask you are there zombies in the new game that's coming." Then to her son, she said, "Why would you want zombies? A lot of dead people stumbling about…"

Aine grinned. "Tell Robbie they're all very keen on zombies, and I saw a drawing of a werewolf."

"There, you see," her mother repeated. "Zombies there are, as well as a werewolf or two. Well," she said to Aine now, "you've made him a happy man. Werewolves indeed."

Listening to her family made Aine feel better. Even though they were thousands of miles away, she could imagine them sitting at the kitchen table over tea, and she wished ferociously that she were there. Safely away from Brady Finn and the temptations he presented.

But as that wish was a useless one, she said only, "I'll think on what you've said, Mum. I promise." Aine stepped out onto the deck, where the wind blew and seabirds cried with a lonesome, mournful sound. "I'll talk to Brady about Danny Leary and then call you again in a day or two."

"Don't worry about calling, love. You do what needs doing and come back to us soon." Her mother paused, then added, "And Robbie says to bring him back a drawing of that werewolf if you can."

"I will." Laughing, Aine hung up, leaned one hand on the cold iron railing and stared out to sea. Right then, Ireland felt a lifetime away, while the lure of Brady Finn was all too close for comfort.

Six

"So what's the deal with you and Irish?" Mike Ryan leaned back in his chair and lifted the bottle of beer for a sip.

"There is no deal," Brady said, studying the label on his beer bottle as if it was a *New York Times* bestseller. The memory of the kiss he'd shared with Aine that afternoon was fresh enough that his blood was still frothing in his veins—not something he felt like sharing. "We're working together on the ideas for the castle and then she goes home. End of story."

"Right," Mike said with a lazy smile. "That's why you go all stone-faced at just the thought of her."

Brady fired a hard look at his friend. Sitting at their usual table in the neighborhood bar, Brady should have been relaxed. Instead, he was anything but. He never should have kissed her, but hell, what man wouldn't have?

Standing there in the wind, that amazing hair blowing about her face and shoulders, those wide green eyes looking up at him. Was he made of granite? Hell no.

Stalling, he looked around the bar. The after-work crowd was all there, with a handful of tourists sprinkled in for good measure. The heavy oak tables gleamed under what was probably a million coats of wax. Overhead lighting made things clear but not overly bright, and the music was low enough that you could enjoy it and still have a conversation. Waitresses in blue denim shorts and yellow T-shirts emblazoned with *Lagoon in Long Beach* weaved in and out of the crowd with the ease of long practice.

He and the Ryans had been coming to the bar since they'd set up shop in the oceanfront Victorian. Right down the street, the location was easy, the bar food was good and they could each catch up on the other's day and compare notes over a cold beer and some hand-cut onion rings. Apparently, though, Brady told himself, work talk wasn't on the menu tonight.

Looking back at Mike, he saw the man's curious expression hadn't abated. He wasn't going to let this go, so Brady made a stab at ending the conversation.

"She's doing the job I want her to do and that's it," he said, grabbing one of the onion rings and crunching down on it.

"Good to know. Okay, then," Mike said, "if there's nothing going on there, you won't mind if I take her out to dinner."

"I mind," Brady said quickly, giving his friend a hard stare. Maybe he was holding back from anything with Aine, but damned if he wanted someone else going after her.

Mike grinned. "Interesting…"

"Stow the grin," Brady told him. "There's nothing going on between us and there won't be with you and her, either. She works for us, Mike."

"It's not the Middle Ages, Brady." Mike laughed and took another sip of beer. "You're not the duke of the castle flirting with the kitchen maid."

Well, that made everything sound ridiculous. Yet he knew that starting up something with an employee was asking for trouble. "Same principle," he insisted.

"Right. With that point of view there'd never be any office romances. Then what would Jamie and Paul in Accounting do?"

"Their *work* for a change?" Brady asked, thinking of the young couple, who were too busy concentrating on each other to pay attention to business half the time.

"Okay, good point," Mike said and leaned forward, snatching one of the onion rings off the platter. "I'm just saying it wouldn't kill you to relax around her a little."

"I'm plenty relaxed." Hell, he was so *relaxed* around Aine he should have been giving off sparks. The only thing that was going to ease the coiled tension in his body was sex. With her. And that was not going to happen.

He'd come here to meet with his partners and maybe take his mind off Aine for a while. So now his only hope was to shift the subject to something Mike didn't want to talk about, either. "Since you're so interested in office romances, what's the deal with you and Jenny Marshall?"

Mike's face went cold and hard. He bit into the onion ring, chewed, then took another swallow of beer before saying, "Like you said about you and Aine. There is no deal. What the hell are you talking about?"

"Sean might be blind," Brady told him, "but I'm not.

I saw the look she sent you when she brought her drawings into the meeting. Hell, your hair should have been on fire."

"Nice. Thanks."

"So what's going on?"

Mike sucked in a gulp of air, scowled at his beer bottle and finally admitted, "About a year ago, we spent some time together, is all."

"Before she came to work for us? Where'd you meet her?"

"At the gaming convention in Phoenix," Mike muttered. "I met her in the bar the night before the con started. Found out the next day she was there running a booth for Snyder's."

"The art program Snyder?"

"Yeah, seems the old man's her uncle." Mike shrugged, but Brady saw the flash of something in his friend's eyes. "She didn't mention that when we met."

"Uh-huh." Okay, good. Subject off Aine and onto something that made Mike look as if he wanted to bite through a rock. Intrigued enough now to take his mind off his own problems for a while, Brady asked, "So what happened?"

"What do you mean what happened?" Mike countered and signaled to the waitress for two more beers. "We met. We said goodbye. Sean hired her and we've been avoiding each other ever since."

"Wow," Brady mused wryly. "It's like a fairy tale."

"Funny." Mike pointed his beer at him. "Don't think I didn't notice how you changed the subject."

"Always said you were the smart Ryan."

"Got that right."

"So why're you avoiding her?"

"Are you writing a book?" Mike asked.

"There's a thought."

"More funny, thanks," Mike grumbled. "Look, it just didn't go anywhere and I don't see the point in pretending we're gonna be friends, because we won't be. I don't like her. She doesn't like me back. Let's leave it at that."

"There's more you're not saying."

"Damn right there is," Mike agreed, then glanced at the door when it swung open and Sean walked in. Quickly, he glanced back at Brady. "As you pointed out, little brother there seems to be blind when it comes to me and Jenny. I'd like to keep him in the dark."

"You quit giving me grief over Aine and it's a deal."

"Done." All smiles now, Mike turned to look at his brother. "You're late and we're out of onion rings. Next round's on you."

"Why's it on me if you two ate them all?" Sean complained, but waved a waitress over.

Brady only half listened to the Ryans as they cheerfully insulted each other. While conversations went on around him, Brady let himself think of Aine again, and had to admit that knowing Mike was having his own problems with a woman made Brady feel just a bit better.

And actually, Mike was in worse shape than Brady. Because Jenny wasn't going anywhere, but soon Aine would be on a plane back to Ireland.

The thought of which didn't make him as happy as it should have.

Two days later, painters were at the office, and so they were holding a meeting in Brady's home. Well, Aine corrected mentally, his penthouse suite in the same hotel she was currently staying in.

She'd never known anyone who actually *lived* in a hotel, and now that she'd seen Brady's place she could safely say she still hadn't. All right, yes, it might be the place he slept in, but there was no real sign of *life*. Oh, the sprawl of rooms was lovely and richly appointed and afforded spectacular views of the coastline. But there was nothing there that indicated it was someone's *home*.

She scrubbed her hands up and down her arms while she wandered the suite. Until they started talking about the castle and what more was to be arranged, she wasn't needed in the conversation. So while the Ryan brothers and Brady argued points of their next game, Aine looked around the palatial space, hoping for insight into Brady Finn. Yet there was nothing. Oh, there was evidence of his wealth in the very fact that he could live here, but there was nothing of his soul. Nothing to scream out, "Brady Finn lives here and these are his things."

Because there were no things. A few books stacked tidily on an end table, three framed photos of him with the Ryans, and beyond that, the place might as well have been standing empty. There were flowers, no doubt delivered by hotel staff. There were lovely paintings on the walls that looked so generic they, too, must have been part of the standard furnishings.

It was lovely but cold. Luxurious but empty. The man had invested nothing of himself in his home. A deliberate choice? She had to wonder if the place he lived was a kind of metaphor for the man himself. Was he only the cold shell he showed the world? Or was there more to the man, hidden away so no one could see?

She thought it was the latter. He was a man who'd closed himself off from emotion, entanglements, and now, knowing he'd had no family to love and be loved by, she could almost understand it. Aine hated that he fascinated her so, because she knew there was no future in it. Beyond the fact that he'd made it clear he wanted nothing more to do with her, she was only in America temporarily. Soon enough she'd be back in Ireland with Brady nothing more than a voice on a phone or a signature on a paycheck.

Yet she couldn't stop thinking about him. That kiss on the pier hadn't helped anything, either. She'd relived that moment countless times in the past couple of days— despite his ridiculous statements after. She'd felt more in those few moments with him than she had with anyone else ever in her life, and so she was left attempting to understand the man who tugged at her heart even when he wasn't trying.

"If the enchanted sword can kill the banshee, then what's the point?" Sean demanded. "It's too easy."

Aine frowned and turned toward the table where all three men stood, bent over the layout of storyboards that Mike had brought to the meeting with him.

"It's not *just* the enchanted sword," Mike argued. "It's not as if you pick it up off the ground and kill the banshee. You have to win the sword first and, you know, the banshee *will* fight back."

"Yeah, but—"

Mike cut his younger brother off. "You also have to navigate through the Burren, avoid the portal tomb, solve the puzzle and find the key that unlocks the damn sword in the first place. It's not easy."

Curious, Aine wandered closer. The Burren was acres and acres of limestone and rock, dotted with grasses and wildflowers. There were rock formations and a view of Galway Bay that drew thousands of tourists a year to the place. Moving in beside Brady so that she could see the drawings spilled across the table, she had the distinct feeling none of the men even noticed her.

"And where's the key going to be hidden again?" Brady asked no one in particular.

Mike sighed. "The key's hidden outside the portal tomb. It's actually *in* the rock itself, but the player has to solve the riddle to find the key or he gets swept into the tomb and transported back to the beginning of the chapter."

"How do you solve the riddle?" Sean asked.

Mike pointed to a series of drawings. "There. John's noted the placement of the clues. There are four. Each clue leads you to a medallion with part of the code. Collect all four, enter the code, get the sword and you can kill the banshee. Otherwise, you're zapped back to the beginning and have to start all over again with no weapons."

"Ooh, that's a nice touch," Sean said, "stripping the player of his weapons."

"It would infuriate my little brother," Aine put in.

Sean grinned at her. "That's what I like to hear."

She shook her head at his obvious pleasure. *What an odd way to make a living*, she thought. Grown men gathered together, discussing banshees and zombies and enchanted swords.

"You can earn more weapons," Mike told her with relish, "but it's going to cost you time, and a real gamer is always looking to set time records."

"I thought Ireland was supposed to be lush and green," Brady said, staring at the images spread before him.

"Mom told us about the Burren," Mike said, "and Joe did the research necessary to make the drawings real. But I think we should let Aine explain the place."

All three men turned to face her, and she reached for one of the drawings depicting the barren moonscape of this little corner of County Clare. "The Burren is about the only place in Ireland that isn't, as you said, green and lush. There's acres of limestone and rock, with many underground caves and tunnels—"

"Hey, we could incorporate caves and tunnels into the player's experience." Sean clapped his hands together and rubbed his palms briskly.

"We could," Brady said. "Let's have Jenny whip up a few bare-bones sketches of tunnels, caves, and how they could tie into the hunting of the banshee."

"Why's it have to be Jenny?" Mike asked.

"Dude," Sean said, "get over it already. She's a terrific artist."

Mike fumed silently and Aine's head whipped back and forth as if she was watching a tennis match as Sean and Brady fed off each other's ideas.

"Anything else, Aine?" Mike asked loudly, getting the other two men to quiet down.

"Nothing specific," she said, smiling. "It's more the feeling you have when you're there, in the midst of that barrenness. It's a haunting place, really. Beautiful in its own way, but raw and wild, as well. Some say if you're there at night, you can hear the cries of the long dead, sobbing into the wind."

"Have you heard them?" Brady asked.

She looked up at him. "I haven't, no. But then I'm not one for crawling about the Burren late at night, either."

Mike grinned. "Haunting. A good description, at least of our version of it. And Sean, let's tell John what Aine just said about the sobs of the dead. See if he can integrate that as background filler through the music."

"So it's sort of a shadow," Brady mused. "I like it."

"Yeah," Sean said. "Me, too. Thanks, Aine. Want a job in the design department?"

"Thank you, no," she countered. "The castle will do me fine. So at the Burren? The werewolves will be there, as well?" she asked, a little sorry to see the stark landscape of the Burren reduced to a habitat for the weird.

"Nah," Sean put in. "Just the banshee, really. Oh, and the ghosts of people she's killed."

"And a zombie or two," Brady put in, pulling another drawing in to show her. "People she's killed but brought back to a half-life to serve her."

Oh, how Robbie would love this, Aine thought, making a face at the image of the rotting zombie. Shaking her head, Aine could only sigh. "Of course, she'd need a servant or two. Even dead ones. And I suppose she rides a pooka?"

"Nice touch," Sean said, clearly loving the idea. He made a quick note on one of the storyboards. "How cool would it be for our banshee to ride a wild pooka? Black horse, red eyes, flames streaming from his mane, black chains hanging off his body just waiting to wrap themselves around unwary travelers…"

Aine laughed and looked up at Brady, charmed to find a real smile on his face as he watched her. How that smile warmed his eyes and touched something deep inside her. Her heart simply turned over in her chest. The man was a mystery, yes, but there was an air about him that made her want to solve the riddle of him. To find what drove him, what touched him. *Foolish woman*, she thought. To want so much from a man she could never have.

For the next few days, Brady focused solely on business and told himself they were both better for it. If he caught confusion in Aine's eyes or regret in his own, he ignored it. Just as he ignored the fact that he wasn't sleeping, because whenever he closed his eyes Aine's features rose up in his mind. Knowing that her hotel room was just five floors down from his wasn't helping the situation.

So he was tired, sexually frustrated and had only himself to blame. If he was anyone else, he'd simply sweep Aine off to bed and release some of the damn tension that had him wired tightly enough to give off sparks. But Brady Finn didn't do complications, and Aine had *complicated* practically stamped on her forehead. She was the kind of woman who would expect happily-ever-after, and since Brady didn't believe in those, he had no business getting involved with her. Besides, she was here temporarily, and when she went back to Ireland, he'd never see her again.

If that thought gave him another pang of regret, he ignored that, as well.

"I've looked at your architect's ideas for expanding the gardens," Aine said, leaning over his desk to point at the sketch she was referring to.

"Problem?" He turned his head to look at her.

Eyes narrowed, she said, "Only that he wants to remove four-hundred-year-old oaks to do the job."

"What?" He scowled at the drawing, then turned to his computer and pulled up the series of photos he had of the castle and the grounds. He was flipping through the pictures looking for the right one when Aine came around his desk and bent down close. Her scent engulfed him and tantalized every breath he drew. Her hair fell, soft and silky against his neck, and he took a short, tight breath in response.

"There, that's it," she said and reached across him,

her breasts pressing against his shoulder as she tapped the computer screen with the tip of her finger. "You see how the trees shade the front of the castle. They've stood centuries, Brady, and to be torn down for a wider lawn, a circular drive, a plot of dahlias and a sign announcing Fate Castle seems a sin."

How the hell was he supposed to care about centuries-old trees when all he could think about was how close she was? How easy it would be to pull her down onto his lap and ease his hunger with another long taste of her? Brady fought down his impulses and focused. She was right. They weren't going to lose the damn trees because a California architect thought a sign would look better in their place.

Because he was speaking through gritted teeth, his voice came out much harsher than he'd meant. "You're right. The trees stay."

"Wonderful," she said, joy in her voice as she straightened up, thank God. She didn't move away, though, merely stood at his side looking down at him.

"Something else?" He hated that his voice sounded strangled and hoped to hell she didn't notice.

"Actually, yes," she said and bit at her bottom lip before saying, "Do you remember when I first got here, we spoke about having Irish workers as part of the crew to do the renovating?"

He frowned, but nodded. "Yeah?"

"Well, a few days ago, I spoke to my mother and she tells me that the people in the village aren't happy with the way things are moving at the castle."

He leaned back in his chair and swiveled around to look at her. Brady felt at a slight disadvantage because he was forced to look up to meet her eyes, so he solved that problem by getting out of his chair to stand. She was close enough to touch, but he didn't. "What're the villagers angry about?"

"It's the American crew, you see," she told him in a rush of words so musical he could have listened to her for hours. "Your man's brought his own people from the States and hasn't made a move to hire locally. The people in the village feel that Irish workers should be having a hand in the work done to our castle."

His eyebrows lifted. "*Your* castle?"

She sniffed and lifted her chin. "As it's been centuries there and you've only just now learned of it, I think it's more ours than yours."

"Except," he reminded her as he perched easily on the edge of his desk, "for the little fact that my partners and I *bought* it."

She waved that aside with a flick of her fingers. "Aye, you paid money for it, but the people in the village and beyond come from those who have fought and died for it. Castle Butler is more than just a hotel to us. It's our past. Our history."

"And if not for me, Sean and Mike, it would be left to rot."

"I'm not arguing that, am I?" she countered reasonably.

"What exactly are you arguing, then? Cut to the bottom line."

"Fine, then. The bottom line, as you put it, is that if you want the support of the village," she said and lifted one finger in a sign to let him know she had more to say, "and you'll *need* that support as you go on, then you'll bend a bit in the remaking of the castle."

"Is that right?" He folded his arms across his chest and said, "Is this some form of Irish blackmail?"

"Not at all," she said quickly, clearly offended. Then her voice softened as well as her eyes. "I'll remind you we talked of this before and you agreed. Brady, don't you see? It's good business. And as you're such an astute businessman, I'm sure you can see the truth of it. If you'll have your man talk to Danny Leary in the village, he can provide as many skilled workmen as are needed."

Brady scowled at her, wondering if all of this was about her securing a job for her boyfriend. "Who's Danny Leary to you? Boyfriend? Lover?"

Stunned, her mouth dropped open and she blinked at him as if she couldn't believe what she'd just heard. Then an instant later, she laughed and shook her head so hard her beautiful hair went flying. "Danny Leary? My lover? His wife would be surprised to hear it—as would his daughter, Kate, who was with me in school."

Well, didn't he feel like an idiot. She was still laughing, and the sound of it dipped inside him and heated him through. The woman was turning him inside out, and the worst of it was she didn't even have to try to accomplish what no other woman ever had.

She was watching him through eyes twinkling with amusement and damned if he could blame her. He was acting like a jealous teenager and he had no right. "Fine," he said abruptly. "I'll contact my crew manager tomorrow and have him get in touch with Danny Leary."

"That's lovely, thanks." She laid one hand on his forearm and he swore he could feel the imprint of her hand burning its way into his skin, right through the shirt fabric. Then her hand dropped away, stealing the heat as it went. "Anyone in the village can tell him where to find Danny."

"I'm sure." For a moment or two, he wondered what it might be like to have the kind of connections that were obviously so important to her. He'd been a loner most of his life—at first through no fault of his own and later by choice. He avoided the very familiarity with people that she seemed to thrive on.

Brady had always felt that life ran much more smoothly when you traveled light. No ties. No strings. The Ryan brothers were the only exception to his rules of living. The only people he'd ever allowed to get close to him. No woman had ever made it past his personal defenses—before Aine.

Desire he understood. Hell, being this close to Aine was pure torture. But love, commitment, those words had no place in Brady's world. And he liked it that way, he reminded himself.

Watching her, Brady asked, "Anything else?"

She pushed one hand through her hair, and Brady tracked that slow, sexy movement. "Not at the moment," she said, "though I was wondering how much longer I'd be here."

Truth be told, she could go home anytime, he thought. They'd done most of what he'd wanted her here for, and the rest could be handled via the internet. But as much as he wanted her gone, he just plain *wanted* her more. So he wasn't ready for her to leave yet, which made no sense at all, since keeping her here was only extending the confusion he felt around her.

"Anxious to be home?"

She turned her head for a quick look out the French doors to the patio beyond. "I'll be sorry to leave this lovely warm weather, but yes. I miss home. Don't you when you travel?"

"No," he said abruptly, stepping back and away from her. "I don't have a home."

"I've never known anyone who lived in a hotel before," she said softly. "Maybe what you need is a place of your own—something less impersonal than the hotel."

He laughed shortly at the idea. Brady just couldn't picture himself mowing a lawn or dealing with nosy neighbors. He wasn't a suburbia kind of guy. "No thanks. The hotel works for me. I can get twenty-four-hour room service, and maids clean the place daily. It's all I need."

"Is it really?"

Defensive now, he said, "We're not all looking for friendly villages." He walked across the room to snatch his jacket off a hanger in the closet. They had a dinner reservation to get to, and he could really use a drink. When she didn't speak, he turned to look at her and frowned when he saw the insult in her eyes.

"No offense," he said, though he knew he'd done just that even without meaning to. "My life is exactly the way I want it to be. How many people can say that?"

"Anyone can say it," she mused, her gaze locked with his. "A better question might be, for how many people is that true?"

He frowned as she passed him and walked through the open door. He didn't much care for the fact that she always got him thinking, reconsidering who he was and what he did. For years, Brady had followed the path he'd laid out for himself, and until Aine Donovan showed up in his life, that path had been straight and smooth. Now there were too many damn bumps.

Staring after her, Brady told himself he'd do well to

not underestimate her, since Aine Donovan had the annoying habit of being able to dig under his skin and stay there. A dangerous woman.

Seven

By the time they left the restaurant after dinner, it was later than Aine might have guessed. Shops were closed, traffic on the street was light and they had the sidewalk to themselves. The air was cool, the breeze brisk, but not as cold as at home. The lightweight dark green sweater she wore over her simple shirt and slacks was enough to keep her warm even as Brady steered her toward his car, parked at the curb.

"Tired?" he asked.

"Not a bit," Aine said. The man nodded but didn't speak. But then he hadn't spoken much during dinner, either. It was the tension, she told herself. As taut as a wire, it hummed between them whenever they were together and only got tighter with every passing day.

"All through dinner you barely spoke," she said as he opened the car door for her. "Is there something wrong?"

"Nothing more than usual," he grumbled, then waved her into the low-slung sports car.

Sighing, Aine slid inside, then buckled her seat belt as she waited for him to join her in the car. The street was nearly empty, which suited her fine. She couldn't quite get used to riding on the wrong side of the street. She was forever flinching or stepping on an imaginary brake.

He climbed in, settled behind the wheel and she asked, "Is it something to do with work?"

"No," he said, jamming the key into the ignition and giving it a twist.

"Is it me, then?" She reached out one hand, laid it on his forearm.

He paused, looked down at her hand, then slowly lifted his gaze to hers. What she saw flaring in his eyes had Aine's heart catching in her chest. Mouth dry, she drew a short, sharp breath and stared into his eyes. She couldn't have looked away if her life had depended on it. For days and days, it had felt as if her blood was at a slow simmer just beneath her skin, and now it began to boil. Slowly, she drew her hand back, and still the raw connection between them remained.

"Yeah," he finally ground out through gritted teeth. "It's you, Aine."

"I don't know what to say."

"Don't say anything," he advised. "Safer that way." He shifted his gaze from her to the street, put the car in gear and it nearly leaped away from the curb. "I promised myself after that kiss that we'd stay away from each other."

"Aye, I remember," she said wryly.

"It's not an easy promise to keep."

Swirls of heat ribboned through her. She liked knowing he was having a difficult time keeping his hands off her. She wished fervently he would stop trying.

Streetlights were a blur as they passed. A light rain left droplets across the windshield that shone like diamonds. The roar of the engine was the only sound and seemed to reverberate through the car. Her fingers curled around the armrest and held on as Brady drove through the night, headed for the hotel.

Minutes later, he was parking his car and holding the door for her. "You don't have to walk me to my room," she said, and her voice sounded rusty, raw.

"I always do. Tonight's no different."

But it was. Everything felt different. She was both nervous and exhilarated. The cool March wind tugged at the edges of her sweater and ruffled her hair, but Brady's hand at the small of her back ensured that she felt nothing but heat. It was a short walk to the hotel and then through the lobby to the elevators.

Once inside the lift, they stepped to opposite sides of the car like opponents in a boxing match, each of them waiting for a bell to ring to bring them together. When the doors opened, Brady pushed away from the wall, took her hand and half dragged her down the well-lit hall to her door. Her skin against his buzzed with sensation. Her stomach swirled and jumped with nerves.

"Key," he said.

She pulled it from her purse and handed it to him as she had every other time he'd brought her home. But this time when her fingers brushed his palm, it was like a match strike against already sensitized skin. She sucked in air like a drowning woman and wondered what would happen once he had her door open.

Was he really planning to leave her? Or would he

come inside? Would he kiss her again? Take her to bed and relieve the nearly painful ache that had been a part of her life for days now?

The door swung open and he didn't move. He stood at her threshold like a man at a crossroads, trying to decide which path to take. After a long moment, he turned his head, looked down at her and said, "I should go."

Disappointment warred with common sense. He should leave, she knew it. To do anything else would be foolish. Crazy even. But, oh, she wanted him to stay.

"Aye," she said at last, surrendering to sanity and putting aside her own wants and needs. "I suppose so."

"Staying would be a mistake," he said, still standing there between in and out.

"It would, no doubt."

"Leaving makes sense."

"It does," she agreed, looking into his eyes, letting him see in hers that she shared the need clawing at him.

He scrubbed one hand across the back of his neck. "Common sense is overrated."

Relief and desire pumped through her all at once, a tangled mix of emotions that left her breathless. "I've thought so myself," she said and went to him when he reached for her.

Sweeping her up in his arms, he held her close, spun them both into her hotel suite and kicked the door shut behind him. Holding her fast, his hands moved up and down her back, sliding low enough to caress her behind and then back up to hold the back of her head while he kissed her until she felt her brain swim.

If they were wrong, Aine couldn't care. Too many days and nights had been spent thinking about this moment. Now that it was here, she didn't want to think at all. This man had slipped into her mind and heart completely, until he was all she thought about. He was cold and generous, lonely and warm and so many confusing things at once that he was mesmerizing.

She held on to him when as a man unhinged, he turned around, leaned her against the wall and ravaged her mouth. Aine gave as well as took, tangling her tongue with his, tasting his breath, his hunger, as well as her own. He threaded his fingers through her hair and held her still as he devoured her. Their heartbeats thundered in time, their bodies burned from the same fire and soon the clothes separating them became a barrier neither could stand for another moment.

He didn't let her go, yet somehow he still managed to strip them out of the clothes that were an irritant. Then they were naked, bodies meshed together while frantic hands swept up and down, exploring, stroking.

Aine'd never felt anything like this. She hadn't known she *could* feel this. Everything that had come before this moment with Brady paled in comparison. She'd had sex before. There'd been Brian, and before him there'd been another, and with both of them the experience had been... pleasant.

Not earth-shattering.

Everywhere Brady touched her, Aine's skin burned, hummed with electricity and energy that pitched and peaked inside her until she thought she might explode with the tension within. And just when she thought she couldn't take it another moment, he made her feel *more*.

Brady's right hand swept down to the juncture of her thighs, cupped her heat, and made Aine's legs collapse. If he hadn't been holding her so tightly, she might have just puddled on the floor. One touch, her mind screamed, just one and she was on the ragged edge of a screaming orgasm. Then he deepened their kiss and at the same time slid two fingers into her heat, stroking and caressing her needy body from the inside.

Impossible sensations flashed into life and she gasped, eyes wide as she let herself go to feel it all. To revel in what he was doing to her. She clung to him, hands curled at his shoulders, mouth fused to his as he pushed her higher and higher. His thumb brushed across the sensitive heart of her and started the cascade of explosions inside her.

That first climax hit Aine so hard, it left her shuddering in his arms and grateful for the strength of him holding her up. She couldn't breathe and didn't care. She was trembling, her skin alive and bristling with the overload of sensations still rumbling through her. And he didn't give her time to savor any of it.

"Again," he murmured, tearing his mouth from hers, dragging his lips along the line of her throat, licking the pulse point in her neck and sending that pulse into a fiercely wild pounding with another touch.

"I can't," she insisted, groaning, tipping her head to one side, to give him better access, to invite more kisses, more nibbling.

"You can." He threaded his fingers through her hair, pulled her head back and stared down into her eyes when he rubbed his thumb across her center.

"Brady!" His talented fingers dazzled her body until every nerve ending was screaming with renewed tension.

He lifted his head to stare down into her passion-glazed eyes. "I've wanted this for days. Wanted *you* for days."

"Me, as well," she said, her voice a strangled whisper.

He pulled her in tightly to him and she felt the hard length of him pressing against her. She groaned, instinctively arching into him, wanting, needing, all of him.

"I can't think about anything but you," he admitted, dipping his head to kiss her shoulder.

Those words floated through her mind like a blessing until he spoke again.

"I don't like it. I don't want to want you." He lifted his head to stare into her eyes. "But I can't stop it."

That should have been a bucket of ice water on her head. Instead, she was contrary enough to take it as a compliment. What better was there than for a strong man to be brought to his knees by a desire he hadn't asked for? Hadn't planned for?

She cupped his face in her palms and gave him her own confession in a breathless voice, and thought what an odd conversation this was to be having while they were naked and his hand was touching her so intimately.

"I'd no more interest in this happening than you, Brady Finn," she said on a sigh. "I'd not thought to find you…this… And yet we're here and I can't find it in me to stop."

"Thank God," he whispered, and took her mouth again like a man seeking the answer to keeping him alive.

She nearly whimpered again when he pulled his hand free of her core, but he gave her no time for thought or regret. Instead, he spun her around and walked her toward the hall. Still kissing, still embracing, the two of them staggered like drunks into the bedroom and fell onto the bed, a tangle of limbs.

She ran her hands up and down his broad back, loving the slide of her skin against his. His body was amazing, strong and yet yielding, and completely and utterly focused on hers. Aine's brain splintered under the on-slaught of sensations pouring through her.

He dipped his head to her breasts and took first one then the other nipple into his mouth. His teeth and tongue tugged at her sensitive skin, and she felt the answering pulls deep within her.

He moved up and down her body, tasting, exploring every inch as if he couldn't get enough of her, and she felt the same. She kissed him when he lowered his mouth to hers and felt the fires engulfing her again. Over and over, he stroked her body until she was nearly frantic with the desperate sort of need she'd never known before. It was as if that first heart-stopping climax hadn't happened at all. Her body was raw and frantic for the next release.

He reared back on his heels, gaze locked with hers and grabbed her hips. Lifting her off the bed to position her just right, he swept into her heat in one long, powerful stroke that had her crying out his name.

She stared into his eyes and couldn't have looked away if it meant her life. She watched as reaction to their join-ing etched itself on his features and thought she'd never seen anything more beautiful than this man in the throes of soul-shattering passion. There was tenderness along with the frantic need. There was intimacy as well as de-sire.

And that was when it hit her. A wild realization she hadn't expected or wanted, but it was undeniable. She'd been wrong before—it wasn't that she was incapable of love; she simply hadn't met the right man until now. Brady Finn was it for her. But how could the right man be the wrong one, as well?

Oh, God help her, she loved him. It wasn't simply pas-sion and desire she felt. She *loved* this man of contradictions. He'd slipped into her heart and she very much feared he was there forever. Aine bit down on her lip to keep from telling him how she felt, as she knew he'd no wish to hear it. Whenever they were together she had the sense that he mentally kept one foot out the door, ready to make his escape before things could become…messy.

And now, she thought, reaching up to touch him, to run her fingertips over his face, down his neck and across his broad, muscular chest, it was too late for her to back away. Maybe it had been from the beginning. All she knew was that the man she loved was inside her, holding her, and that was enough.

As her body coiled into a tightened spring, Brady set a rhythm that she raced to match. Locking her legs around his hips, she pulled him higher and tighter at his every thrust. She wanted to hold him close enough that she'd never lose him. Her nails scored his back, her breath chugged out of her lungs and her head tipped back into the cool silk of the pillow beneath her.

"Look at me," he ordered, his voice hardly more than a low growl of desperation. "I want to watch your eyes as I take you."

Aine looked up at him, gaze locking with his. It took all she had to keep from whispering, "I love you," as her body simply imploded with another orgasm so strong that shards of pleasure slid brokenly through her veins. She couldn't look away from those shining blue eyes staring into hers. She clung to him, continuing to move her hips in time with his. Then he flipped her over until she straddled him and his body slid even higher into hers.

"Oh, my…" Her head fell back. His hands gripped her hips and guided her as she rocked on him, holding him deeply inside her. The glory of it filled her as completely as he did. There was something here, something rich and meaningful and desperately beautiful.

"Brady…" She looked down into his eyes and saw the flash of passion erupt, and a moment later felt his powerful body arch and tremble as he surrendered to the inevitable and emptied himself inside her.

Brady couldn't remember the last time he'd let himself lose control like that. His body still humming with a damn near electrical buzz, he wrapped his arms around the woman sprawled across his chest. She'd shattered him. Pushed him beyond the edges of control.

His world was in pieces around him. She'd splintered his preconceptions and left him wondering what the hell had happened to him. For the first time in memory, he'd lost every ounce of self-discipline he'd spent a lifetime acquiring. Losing himself in her was something he hadn't counted on. Hell, he hadn't been that careless, that hungry with a woman since he was a kid. There'd been no seduction here. No romance, no soft sighs and tender touches. Just need. Hunger.

"Considering what's just happened, you don't look very happy." She folded her arms across his chest and looked down at him.

"Yeah." His body was plenty happy. It was his mind that wouldn't give him any peace. Brady rolled to one side so she could stretch out on the mattress beside him. "Did I hurt you?"

He'd been rough and hadn't intended to be, and that was lowering. But then, he hadn't intended any of this to happen, so that made sense in a bizarre sort of way.

"Of course you didn't hurt me," Aine said, reaching

out to smooth his hair back from his face. "What is it that's worrying you so?"

The cool skim of her fingertips against his skin was more than he could take. He caught her hand and held it still. If she kept touching him, he'd have her again, because the need for her hadn't ended as he'd hoped, but only grown. His gaze on hers now, he saw her smile and wondered how she could be so easy with what had just happened between them.

"What is it?" Brady went up on one elbow and stared down at her. "I practically forced you to—"

He broke off when she laughed. Ordinarily that musical, Irish-flavored sound would have ignited a fire inside him. Now it just astounded him.

Reaching up, she slid one hand up and down his arm. "I'm sorry, really. But to say I was nearly forced when I tore your clothes off you is really a bit much, wouldn't you agree?"

"Okay, yes. You're right." But that didn't change the fact that he'd broken his own personal creed about getting involved with an employee. Worse, one who was far from home and probably more vulnerable than even she was aware.

It wasn't only that burrowing through his mind, though, and Brady knew it. He'd allowed Aine to get close. Closer than anyone else ever had. She'd blinded him to everything but her, and he was still overwhelmed by all of it.

"I still shouldn't have—"

"What?" she asked, grinning as she pushed her hair back from her face and sighed a little. "Used me so completely and thoroughly? If you think to apologize for that, I'll tell you now there's no need. I don't bruise easily, and if I hadn't been interested, I'm quite capable of saying no." A contented sigh slipped from her. "As it is, I think we both did a fine job of it, don't you?"

He stared at her. This had to be the weirdest after-sex conversation he'd ever had. Of course Aine Donovan would prove to be just as confusing in bed as she was out of it. Just another reason, he thought, to cut ties, to back away. She intrigued him constantly and she was already taking up way too many of his thoughts.

"You've still a frown on your face," she pointed out.

"I don't know what to make of you," Brady admitted, scowling at the admission he hadn't meant to make.

"That's lovely," she said with a pleased smile. "Thank you."

"Wasn't a compliment."

She shrugged. "I'll think of it as one, if it's all the same to you."

Darkness crept into the room inch by inch. Her eyes were in shadow now, so he couldn't try to read them as he shared the real worry about this evening. The cost of his lack of self-control that clearly she hadn't thought of yet. Damn it, Brady had built a life around responsibility, around being in control of himself and everything around him. Never once had he risked the life he'd built by being reckless. Until tonight. Knowing that he'd thrown all of that away in a moment of passion made him furious with himself.

Staring at her, he said, "All right, well, think of this, too. We were both too busy to notice we didn't use protection."

Aine paled, bolted upright, turned to the bedside table and flipped the lamp on. Shadows fled instantly, and when she looked at Brady she could see him blinking at the sudden bright light. He had taken her to heaven only to send her crashing back to earth with a thud.

Seconds ago she'd been thinking that love had sneaked up on her. That falling for Brady Finn had been inevitable. That it didn't matter if she couldn't have him; it was enough just to know that she loved. That she'd found something most people never knew.

Now...there was more. She was both terrified and oddly hopeful. Which went to show, she guessed, just how muddled her thinking was at the moment.

"So," he said wryly, "*now* you see why I'm frowning."

"Aye, I do." Her stomach did a quick flip and her mind raced as she realized the possible ramifications of what had happened between her and Brady. She would be leaving soon. Going home to a job, a family and a country that she loved. And what if she was pregnant? What then?

Oh, she couldn't wrap her mind around it.

Too many thoughts circled her brain like sharks, each taking a nibble, each demanding to be noticed. Yet how could she make sense of anything? *Pregnant?* Sliding off the bed, she dragged the duvet off the end of the mattress to wrap around her naked body. Holding it to her like a colorful, fluffy shield, she walked to the wide windows, then spun around and came back to the bed again. Whatever she might have said went unuttered when he spoke first.

"I wasn't thinking," Brady told her, and looked as though he'd rather bite off his own tongue than say what he added next. "Not since high school have I been so wrapped up in a woman that I forgot a damn condom."

Aine would have smiled at that, because really, it was a lovely compliment. She could say the same, of course, but as he was so busy heaping coals on his own head she didn't think he'd care to hear it. So she would give him what he needed. Calm. Cool. Deliberate.

"Well, then," she said firmly, tightening her grasp on the duvet, "what's done is done, so there's no use fretting over what can't be changed."

"Fretting?" He pushed off the bed and stalked toward her, apparently completely comfortable being naked.

He was magnificent, was all she could think. Tanned and strong, and a ferocious look on his features that had her heart clutching in her chest and her breath staggering in odd little gasps.

Gripping her upper arms, he asked, "That's what you think I'm doing? *Fretting?*"

"Of course not. I understand you're upset. As am I. But what more is there to do about it?" she asked, shaking her head. "The horse is gone, so 'tis useless now to worry about locking the barn door."

"Barn doors and horses," he muttered darkly. "You're damn right it's too late now. But we need to talk about what might happen."

"Don't curse at me," she said and pulled free of his grip. "We both know what might happen. Do you need me to say it? Then I will. I might be pregnant."

Oh, just saying that word aloud made her knees tremble. Wishful thinking be blasted. How could she have been so foolish? So utterly careless? It wasn't as if she were a shy virgin and this was her first time with a man. She was smart, capable and, right now, shaken to the core at what they'd done. But she wouldn't show him just how unsettled she was. She'd her pride after all.

"What else is there to say?" she asked, lifting one hand in an eloquent shrug.

"Plenty," he muttered, then turned and walked out of the room. "A man can't have this kind of conversation naked."

While he was gone, she took several deep breaths to steady her nerves. It didn't really help. Her heartbeat skittered unsteadily, and when he came back he found her exactly where he'd left her. "If you're pregnant…"

"That's a big if, if you don't mind my saying."

"Why aren't you upset?" he demanded, eyes narrowed on her.

She was, but there was a small part of her deep inside that wondered, would it really be so bad if she *were* pregnant? True, it wouldn't be a perfect situation, but she'd always wanted a family. *Crazy.* Looking at Brady, though, she knew he would never see a baby as a happy accident. He was too busy railing against circumstances.

"Because it would do no good to be upset," she said quietly. "Would you rather I weep and wail, perhaps keen a bit like the banshees you seem so fond of?"

"That would make more sense," he admitted, throwing both hands high.

His frustration was nearly palpable. He was a man used to being in control, and so this had to be hard for him. She sympathized, but for her, there was simply no point in anguish before she knew if there was a reason for it. Brady might be used to ordering his world to follow his commands, but Aine was more accustomed to things spiraling *out* of her control.

"To you, perhaps," she said softly. "But it's not my way."

"What *is* your way, Aine?"

"To wait and see, of course. There's no point in worrying a bone before you have one, is there?" She pushed her hair back in an impatient gesture. "There's an old Irish saying. 'If you worry, you die. If you don't worry, you die. So why worry?'"

"What the hell does that *mean*?" he shouted.

"Not to worry! Weren't you listening?" Aine felt her own temper bubble and strain at the leash she had it on. Deliberately, she took another breath and told herself to calm down. "It was only the one time, Brady. I hardly think it's worth this much concern."

"It only takes once," he reminded her tightly.

"Aye," she said, "in books and movies." Shaking her head, she continued, "I've a friend back home who tried for four years to get pregnant. Real life isn't as predictable as fiction, so it's a waste to think it is."

"Wishful thinking's pretty much a waste, too."

Strange, she thought, that his "wishful thinking" was hoping she wasn't pregnant and her own was not as appalled at the idea of a baby as it should be. But planned for or not, a child would be a gift, and she refused to see it as anything else.

He stuffed his hands into the pockets of his slacks, inadvertently tugging them down farther over his abdomen. The man was too handsome by far, and as she watched him, Aine thought again that he could have been a pirate with that sharp gleam in his eyes and the tight scowl on his lips.

The silence between them stretched out into long, uncomfortable seconds that seemed to take on a life of their own. How could they have been so close only minutes ago and now seem as though they were separated by thousands of miles? When she couldn't stand it anymore, Aine took one long step toward him. Reaching out, she laid one hand on his forearm and said, "This isn't help-ing, Brady."

At her touch, he went as stiff as stone and his features as blank as any marble statue. Why was she suddenly so cold? Was it the ice in his eyes?

Moving away, as if he couldn't bear to be next to her for another minute, Brady began to pace the confines of the room like a trapped animal looking desperately for a way out. Aine's heart hurt at the image. Even after what they'd just shared, he was anxious to be away from her.

"You're right," he finally said. "It's not helping. There's only one thing that will." He pushed one hand through his hair and threw her a quick glance.

Aine buried her hurt. He was regretting what they'd found together. And maybe she should be, too. But Aine knew that no matter what happened next, she would never second-guess lying with Brady Finn. She'd discovered her love for him and found more pleasure in his arms than she'd ever known before. She couldn't regret it, even knowing that nothing could come of it.

Still, she lifted her chin, kept a tight grip on the duvet she still held to herself and waited for him to speak again. She was determined not to let him see what she was feel-ing. To keep to herself the fact that his reaction to all of this was tearing at her heart.

The man was cool and deliberate, as distant as he'd been when she first met him. It was as if the Brady she'd come to know had vanished. When he spoke, she was sure of it.

"I think it's time you went back to Ireland."

"What?" She simply stared at him.

He stopped dead, crossed his arms over his chest and

braced his bare feet wide apart. "You wanted to go home. I think you should. Right away."

"That's your answer to tonight?" she asked, hardly believing what he was saying. Yes, she would have gone back home in a week or so anyway, but this felt as if he was throwing her out of the country simply to avoid an awkward situation. "To send me away?"

"Don't make this more than it is," he snapped, then caught himself and took a breath. "Tonight's got nothing to do with it. You did a good job. Now it's time to go home. With a raise."

"A raise, is it?" Her voice sounded as thin and sharp as a blade, yet she couldn't seem to change it. With her heart in her throat it was a wonder she could get any words out at all. If he'd slapped her she couldn't have been more shocked.

Rage and pain twisted into tight knots in the pit of her stomach. She was being dismissed, was all she could think. He was throwing money at her as if to buy her silence about what had happened between them. Or worse yet, as if she were nothing more than a passing fancy who could be bought off with the ease of writing a check.

Her cheeks flushed with heat. She felt it and knew it was the result of being treated as if she was disposable. A mistake to be quickly erased and forgotten. Shame rose up to choke her, then spilled out in a rush of words.

"I did a good job?" she repeated. "Where do you mean? On the castle or right here?" She waved one hand at the rumpled bed.

"You're putting words in my mouth again."

"There's no need. You were plain enough. You think I'm to be bought off, is that it?" She didn't wait for an answer, just swept on, riding the tide of her own fury.

"Though I'm your employee, I'm no servant to be sent off for getting too close to the master of the house."

He scowled at her, his brows lowering dangerously. "What the hell are you talking about now? This isn't about us sleeping together."

"Of course it is," she shouted. "Let's be honest here at least."

"How is giving you a raise and sending you home an insult?"

"You know very well," she said, kicking the duvet out of her way and stalking toward him. "You've decided to rid yourself of me in the most expedient way. Am I to be grateful, then, for this *raise* you're dangling in front of me?"

"If you don't want the damn raise, don't take it," he told her, staring down at her. "And you're not a damn servant. Having sex was a mistake. We both knew going in that it would be, Aine. I'm just trying to do what's best for both of us."

How could his eyes be so cold when only minutes earlier they'd burned with passion? And how could she feel so alone standing right in front of the man she loved?

"If you'd calm down and think," he advised tightly, "you'd see that this is the only solution. You were never staying here anyway, and to stay longer now would just be…awkward."

"Aye," she whispered. "It would be, wouldn't it? Having a temporary lover about might be problematic. Especially if you have your eye already on your next temporary lover."

He blew out a breath and scrubbed both hands over his face. "This isn't about the sex. I'm not looking for a lover and I'm not throwing you into a dungeon, for God's sake—I'm sending you *home*. The home you said you missed. Well, now you don't have to miss it."

"Oh, I'm sure I'll be *grateful* as soon as I calm down and think."

He winced when she threw his words back at him. Then Brady reached for her, but Aine scuttled backward, because she knew she couldn't bear it if he touched her. She was sure she would simply shatter like a crystal vase dropped on stone.

"So it's as it was after that first kiss. It's *you* who decides what the 'right thing' to do is."

"Are you actually trying to tell me this wasn't a mistake?" he asked.

"I'll not try to tell you anything," Aine said softly. It hadn't felt like a mistake. It had been a revelation. At least for her. She'd found love, *finally*, and now the man she loved was looking at her as though he regretted ever meeting her. "What would be the point?"

"Aine…"

"Please leave." She wanted—no needed—to be alone. Aine couldn't bear the thought of him seeing her cry, and tears were so close to the surface now it was all she could do to hold them back. "I'll go home, and gladly. I'll send you reports on the castle's progress, and I'll earn every penny of the raise you've offered."

"And you'll tell me if you're pregnant."

His voice was hard now and as distant as the moon. She felt his absence as if he'd already left, because she knew in his heart he had.

"I'll do that." She wouldn't, though. He'd made himself clear enough, hadn't he? He'd no interest in her, so why would he care about a child that came from her? No, this time with Brady was done. Their connection, if they'd ever really had one outside her own idle day-dreams, was over.

Without a word more, he walked past her. She watched him leave and didn't speak. She heard him gather his clothes, let himself out of the suite and close the door behind him and still she stood alone in the shadows. She expected the tears to come then, but they didn't.

They were as frozen as her heart.

Eight

Five months later...

"How long are you gonna be in Ireland?"

Brady looked over at Mike and shrugged. "Shouldn't be long. I just want to check on the progress being made."

"Uh-huh." Mike sat back in his chair and lifted his feet to the edge of Brady's desk, crossing his legs at the ankle.

Brady stifled an impatient sigh. It had been five months since he'd last seen Aine. Five months of emails and short, terse phone calls once a week. True to her word, she'd kept him up-to-date on the renovation and according to her, everything was on schedule. So there was no real reason for him to fly to Ireland—and Mike knew it. So naturally, his friend had to rag him about it.

"It's a business trip," Brady said, stacking the last of the papers on his desk before tucking them away in the top drawer. "That's it."

"Right. This from the same man who said a few months back that with the 360-degree videos there was no reason to go to Ireland in person."

"That was before the renovations started," Brady argued.

"Did Aine say there was a problem?"

"No." In fact, she never said much at all. Irritation simmered deep in his gut. Her emails were rarely more than a sentence or two long. She called once a week without fail, and he could feel the ice in her voice despite the thousands of miles separating them. As far as work went, he had nothing to complain about. She was businesslike and organized and so damn far away it was driving him nuts.

The memory of that last night with her rose up in his mind suddenly, and he could see her as clearly as if she were in the room with him. Her eyes wide and wounded, her hair tumbling around her shoulders in a wild dark red tangle and the duvet she'd held to herself while she'd stared at him in shock.

Hell, it had all gone downhill so fast. The next morning, she had come into the offices, said goodbye to everyone and left for home that afternoon. In a blink it was as if she had never been there at all. Except for the fact that he couldn't go more than an hour without thinking about her.

Then there had been the awkward phone call a few months ago when he'd asked if she was pregnant and she'd told him he had nothing to worry about. He'd almost been disappointed—if there'd been a baby, he'd have had an excuse for seeing her again. But the reality was it was better this way since he knew nothing about being a father. How could he know when he'd never *had* a father?

"So there's no problem, but you're still hopping a jet." Mike grinned. "Why don't you just admit you miss her?"

Because he didn't miss her. That was ridiculous. Brady Finn didn't get close enough to women to miss them when they were gone. Maybe he hadn't been with anyone else since she'd left, but that was because he'd been busy. It had nothing to do with the fact that he could still hear her voice, musical with the sound of Ireland. That he could still see her eyes, as green as a forest. That her taste was still inside him, smothering any other needs in his continuing hunger for her. No, he didn't miss her. He just needed to see her again to clear his mind and then he could return to his life. That was what this was about, he assured himself. Closure.

He needed to look into her eyes, say a clean goodbye and then leave again with a clear conscience. He didn't want the memory of her hurt and insult in his mind anymore.

"Missing a woman isn't a crime, you know."

Brady stiffened, then shot Mike another look. "I don't miss her. I talk to her once a week, don't I? Look, she works for us," he said reasonably. "I'm going to check on the hotel I'm in charge of remodeling. It's business, Mike. That's it."

His friend snorted, dropped his feet to the floor and stood up. Shoving both hands into his pockets, Mike said, "If you really believe that, you are some kind of sad, my friend." He turned and strolled to the door. When he got there, he glanced over his shoulder and said, "If you're just lying to yourself, then good luck with that."

Brady didn't need luck. All he was going to do was check out the castle, make sure the work was going well. Seeing Aine—was Mike right? *Was* he lying to himself?

Brady scrubbed both hands over his face and grumbled, "Damn it, Mike, stay the hell out of my head."

His friend's laughter floated to him from the hallway.

Aine loved her family. She really did. But since she'd moved into one of the bedrooms at the castle and had her own space, it was much easier to love them. Her mother and Robbie had been nothing but supportive since her return home. She'd slipped back into her life almost as if California hadn't happened. Almost. She'd been raw and hurt and sick to her soul when she came home and echoes of that pain were still with her.

But working at the castle kept her busy enough that most of the time Aine could push thoughts of Brady Finn to the back of her mind. It was only the nights that were crowded with memories of him. When she couldn't sleep for thoughts of him, Aine would wander the halls of Castle Butler and have to admit that Brady Finn was doing something wonderful here.

Despite the hurt she felt when thoughts of him settled in her mind and heart, Aine could see the difference in the castle and almost see what it would be when finished. The changes were many, some subtle, some outrageous, but the castle itself remained strong, a reminder to her that whatever changes she faced, she, too, could overcome them.

"But don't take that the wrong way, love," Aine said, sliding her palm across the rounded bulge of her belly. "You're a change I'm looking forward to."

Five months' pregnant and unmarried, some might think she'd be in a panic. But she wasn't. Certainly she worried a bit about the future, as being a single mother was a frightening situation. Still, she was twenty-eight years old and didn't care about village gossip a bit. Her family loved her and she had a good job, a place to live and, in a few short months, she would have a living connection to the man she had loved…and lost.

Aine shrugged deeper into the heavy cream-colored Irish-knit sweater she wore and stuffed both hands into the pockets. She walked downstairs to check on the workmen already making a storm of noise, and while she went thoughts of Brady once more drifted through her mind.

Odd that she'd gone her whole life without feeling these conflicting emotions. She'd been engaged, and had never once felt the swift tugs and pulls that Brady engendered in her. Why was it the man she wanted most was the one man she could never have? Why was he so determined to pull away and shut himself off from any kind of real love and connection?

That was why she hadn't told him about the baby. He was so determined to be alone, so convinced he needed no one, she knew he wouldn't want to be a father to her child. Oh, he would do the dutiful thing, she'd no doubt. He had integrity aplenty, and he would once again sacrifice himself because it was the "right" thing to do. But she needed no sacrificial saint to help raise her child. If he couldn't offer love, he had nothing she and her baby needed.

"Aine, love," Danny Leary called to her from the far side of the banquet room. "Have you been to the kitchen yet today?"

Danny was built like the trunk of one of the ancient oaks surrounding the castle, though coming in much shorter. He was thick with muscles gained from years of hard work. His gray hair was cut short, his blue eyes as sharp as diamonds. He was strong as a bear and gentle as a lamb and one of her late father's oldest friends.

"No," she said, determinedly pushing thoughts of Brady aside. "Why?"

"We've a decision to make there." Danny shifted the hammer he held from hand to hand. "The new stove's arrived, and it's too wide to fit."

She sighed and buried a quick flash of temper at the latest annoyance. "Who did the measurements?"

"I did them myself and they were good, but the company's made a mistake. So now," he said with a shake of his head, "you've a choice. We can have them ship it back and send out another, but the time delay will hold off the painting, the new counters and the new flooring, as well."

Not a catastrophe by any means, just one more bump in a road that had proved itself to have plenty of ruts in it. "What has to be done to make it work?"

He grinned. "If we take out one of the lower cabinets, she'll slide in as if the spot were made for her. And this stove's two more burners on it than the one ordered in the first place, so it could be a blessing in disguise."

"Let's have it, then," she said, making the decision on the spot. "I trust you to do the job right."

"There's a girl," Danny said and winked at her. "Now, then, there's something else, as the slate tiles for the roof have been delayed again."

Her shoulders slumped. It had been months now they'd waited for those tiles. They'd had to be specially made, to keep with the medieval feel of the castle. But with this latest delay it pushed back the renovation of the rooms on the top floor. No one could redo floors and walls and then have rain come through the holes in the roof and ruin everything.

"I'll call them again."

"Good. You could also call about the flagstones for the garden, as they arrived broken and will have to be replaced."

"For pity's sake," she muttered, and pulled her phone from her pocket, making notes on who to call next. It seemed always there was one problem after another.

But Danny wasn't finished. "Now, if you've another moment or two, Kevin Reilly could use your decision on the paint color for the washrooms off the main lobby."

Aine nodded and walked off in that direction. It felt as though she walked miles every day, from one end of the castle to the other. Her steps matched the rhythm set by the crack of hammers and the buzz of saws, not to mention the traditional music pumping from a radio tucked on a ladder nearby. Everyone had a purpose, and Brady's dream was happening before her eyes.

The banquet room was nearly finished, with its tapestries hung, the oversize mantel carved and in place over the refurbished stone hearth. There were what looked to be mile-long tables with benches drawn up to them. Leaded windows let in the watery sunlight peeking through storm clouds, and the refinished floors were covered by protective tarps. She felt the castle coming to life in a way she'd never expected. The murals in the banquet room were otherworldly, true, but they were also beautiful. She shouldn't have worried on that score. Brady had been right—she'd have to remember to tell him that when she made her weekly progress report call tomorrow.

Talking to him every week was getting harder, because as the baby grew and stirred inside her, it felt more and more as though she was cheating him. Her heart urged her to tell him he was to be a father, but her mind kept insisting he wouldn't want to know. And Aine couldn't bear to hear him make excuses—or worse yet, offer her duty when what she wanted was love. So she would keep her secrets and her memories to herself.

The road was so narrow that if another car came at him, Brady thought, he'd just have to die. There was no room to pull over. The thick hedges Aine had told him about crouched so close to the narrow track he drove along, they actually scraped against his impossibly small rental car at nearly every turn.

Brady checked the GPS on his phone and knew he was less than twenty minutes from the castle. His blood hummed in anticipation. It wasn't the damn castle he was interested in seeing, it was Aine. The deeper he drove into her country, the sharper the memories of her became. Her voice. Her smile. That quick flash of temper that disappeared as fast as it erupted.

He'd thought that sending her home would get her out of his thoughts, but instead, the opposite had happened. When he couldn't see her, his brain provided a stockpile of images to make sure he didn't forget her. But memory was a tricky thing, he knew, and he was sure that somehow his own brain was making her seem more than she really was. This trip would settle it. Would show him that she was just another woman and then he could move the hell on and leave her behind.

The car crested a hill, and it seemed that all of Ireland opened up in front of him. A wide sweep of valley so green it hurt to look at it. Stone fences threaded through the green like gray ribbon, and a few scattered cottages looked as though they'd been plunked down in the middle of a painting. Cows and sheep dotted the fields, and not far off, a farmer rode a tractor, churning up black earth. Sunlight speared through the clouds and lay like gold across the fields. The sky was as blue as Aine had promised, and the distant sea glittered darkly like a sapphire.

Even better, Brady spotted the hulking shadow of the castle not far off. In a few minutes, he was driving through the entry, making a mental note to have the tall metal gates painted. On the right stood the guest cottage where Aine lived with her family. He almost stopped, then decided to go to the castle first, then find his hotel manager.

It was impressive, was all he could think as he parked the car in front of the wide double doors. The three-story building was gray stone that contained enough mica to make it glitter when the sun slanted across it. He did a slow turn, taking in the whole picture, and had to admit that it was a different thing entirely to actually stand in front of the castle than it had been to see the pictures of it. A cold wind sliced at him, belying the fact that it was August. The wide lawn was trimmed, the ancient oaks provided shade for the castle entrance and flowers in the neatly tended beds dipped and swayed in a wind that carried the scent of the sea.

He hadn't expected it all to be so beautiful. Or to feel almost...*familiar*. Which just went to prove that jet lag had set in.

Behind him, the front door opened and Brady turned around to see a short barrel-chested man with gray hair and sharp blue eyes glaring at him.

"You've come, then," the man said with a brisk nod. "And about time if you're asking me."

"I'm sorry?"

"It's not my pardon you should be begging, is it?"

Irritation stirred. "What're you talking about?"

"I'm talking man-to-man about what's decent, aren't I? You'll be Brady Finn." The man came down the steps like a bull chasing down an intruder in his field. "I know your face from the pictures Aine showed me."

Brady looked down at the much shorter man. "Who're you?"

"Danny Leary," he said and didn't offer his hand. "I'm one of those putting the castle to rights."

So this was the man Aine had gone to bat for. "Aine told me about you," Brady said and didn't add that she hadn't mentioned he was a little nuts.

"Did she, now? Well, she told all of us about you as well, Brady Finn, and as I said, it's high time you showed yourself." Danny propped fists on his hips, scowled up at Brady and said, "As her father, God rest him, was my friend, I'll stand for him now. You've been too long in coming, but as you're here now, we'll settle this for good and all."

"Settle *what*?" Brady was tired, hungry and in no mood for playing games. Besides all that, he wasn't used to having his employees chew him out as though he was ten years old.

A storm cloud settled on the older man's features. "Follow me, then." Danny turned and charged back up the stairs, not bothering to see if Brady came after him or not.

He followed the man into the castle and stopped dead in the entryway. A wall of noise greeted him. Saws, hammers, men shouting, music playing. The place was huge, so the sound ricocheted off the cathedral ceiling and slammed back down to crash into Brady's head. Gray stone walls were dotted with pennants, tapestries and broadswords. Leaded windows allowed sunlight to spear into the open space. He could see the wide staircase off to the right, its ancient stone steps covered by a deep red runner. A highly polished, intricately carved wooden banister gleamed in the light.

"Aine!" Danny shouted from off to Brady's left. "What're you doing on that ladder, lass? You've no business climbing that thing."

Brady walked into what was clearly the banquet hall. In a split second, his gaze swept the room and he was impressed. It was exactly as he'd imagined it. The feel of the Middle Ages and the comfort of the twenty-first century. Perfect. Right down to the paintings of warriors, werewolves and banshees on the walls.

"Come on down now and careful," the man was saying. "Mind your step, lass."

"I'm fine, Danny," she said on a laugh, "I was just putting a new bulb in this sconce. What do you think? A lower wattage looks more like torchlight, but 'tisn't as bright as a higher-watt bulb."

"I like the torch idea myself," Danny answered.

"As do I."

The musical voice that had haunted Brady for five months fisted something inside him. He watched as Danny helped her down the last few rungs of a ladder and couldn't take his eyes off her. She hadn't seen him yet, so he took advantage of the moment to indulge himself by letting his gaze sweep over her. That amazing hair of hers hung loose in waves and curls of dark fire that fell around her shoulders. She wore a thick sweater over jeans and boots, and Brady thought he'd never seen anything so beautiful.

Damn, he'd missed her. Hadn't wanted to. Had tried

to talk himself out of it time and again, yet she hadn't left his mind once over the past five months.

"Danny," she was saying, "you don't have to worry about me."

"I've known you all your life, lass. And if you haven't the sense to know a pregnant woman has no business climbing a ladder, what choice do I have but to worry?"

"Pregnant?"

Aine whirled around so fast, her hair swung out in an arc around her head. Her face was pale, her green eyes wide and startled. But all he could see was the rounded belly defined by a tight yellow shirt exposed when her sweater swung open. "Brady? What're you doing here?"

"You're pregnant?" he demanded. "What the hell, Aine?"

"Don't curse at me," she snapped.

"He didn't *know*?" Danny bellowed. "You've kept it from the man all this time?"

"No," Brady ground out, answering Danny's question himself. "I didn't know. She didn't bother to tell me."

His gaze drilled into Aine's, and he had some small satisfaction in seeing shame flicker briefly in her eyes. It felt as if there was a giant iron band wrapped around his chest, slowly tightening until he could hardly breathe. His brain was racing and was still outpaced by the damn anger that had him by the throat.

"How could you not tell the man he's to be a father?"

Aine shot Danny a look. "I've my reasons."

"I'm sure they're great ones," Brady snapped. "Can't wait to hear 'em."

Danny folded his arms across his broad chest. "I'd like to know that, as well."

"What were you waiting for, Aine?" Brady took a step

closer and forced himself to stop. "When the kid needs college money?"

Little by little, Brady noticed, the noise in the castle was beginning to die off. First it was the saw, then the hammers. Music, though, still pumped through the air, and a few men shouted to be heard over it.

Aine sucked in a gulp of air and fired a furious look at him. "Did I ever ask you for anything?" she demanded, clearly outraged. "How can you say I'd come to you for *money*?"

"Aye, that was a bit harsh," Danny put in.

Brady wasn't listening. "What else am I supposed to think? You don't tell me you're pregnant and I'm supposed to, what? Congratulate you on your integrity and honesty?"

Her incredible green eyes narrowed and a splash of temper appeared on her pale cheeks. "You've no call to question my honesty."

Brady waved one hand at her belly. "Looks as if I've got about five months' worth of reason."

"Well, he has you there, love," Danny said.

Now the quiet in the castle was nearly ghostly. The silence was so profound, Brady was sure he could hear his own heart crashing in his chest.

A *father*? He'd spent his entire adult life avoiding just this situation, and all it had taken was one night of forgetting—one night of incredible sex mixed with a lack of control—to plunk him right in the middle of it. He couldn't sort through the dozens of emotions and reactions racing through him. All he could think was he was a *father*. And hell if he knew what to do about it.

Vaguely, he noticed the banquet room filling with curious people. One by one, men came in from wherever they'd been working, following the sounds of shouting. They stood in a wary half circle, waiting for the argument to continue. And for the first time, Brady came to himself long enough to realize he was discussing damned private things with a damn audience.

"That's it for the show," he announced, his voice deep and dark and loud enough to carry throughout the castle. "You men get back to work—"

"Who's he to be ordering us about?" someone whispered.

"He's your boss, Jack Dooley," Danny said loudly enough to cover any other questions. "And he's right and all. Back to work, the lot of you." Then the older man gave Brady a nod and a wink before joining the rest of the crew in their slow shuffle out of the room.

Stalking across the few feet of space separating him from Aine, Brady grabbed her upper arm in a tight grip and fought to ignore the expected flare of heat that zipped from her to him and back again. "We'll finish this in private."

She pulled away and said, "There's nothing to finish."

Brady laughed shortly, but there was no humor in it. "You can't be serious."

"Fine. We'll go upstairs to my room."

"Your room? I thought you lived in the guest cottage."

"I moved into the castle some time ago, to better keep an eye on things as they happen." She walked past him, chin lifted, head held high. Like a damn queen, Brady told himself and followed after, the sound of his footsteps echoing loudly in the quiet.

"You'll notice the work on the ground floor's progressing," she said, voice thin and tight, like a bored tour guide. "The first floor—second to you—is nearly finished as well, but the top floor's another matter entirely."

He was hardly listening. In spite of the anger rushing through him he was distracted by the sway of her behind as she climbed the stairs. Gritting his teeth, he looked away and when he did, he noticed some of the work done on the place. At the landing, thick bloodred carpets ran the length of the hallway, and pewter sconces chased away gloomy day shadows. Paintings based on the "Fate Castle" game were framed and hung, and he lost a moment or two admiring them.

"It looks good," he said, grudgingly.

"It does." She turned to the right and walked down the hall to the room at the far end, where she opened the door and Brady followed her inside.

The room was big, filled with antiques and boasting a window seat. There was a fireplace, two chairs pulled up in front of it. A heavy wooden chest sat at the end of a massive four-poster bed opposite a wide flat-screen television hanging over the hearth.

Brady walked to the window, pulled the drapes aside and looked down on what appeared to be a maze. He didn't give a damn about the scenery, though he was only trying to ease the tightness in his chest, get a grip on his anger. But that wasn't working, so he thought, *Screw it*, and turned around to face Aine.

His heart felt as if a tight fist were closed around it, and even with that, his body stirred at the sight of her. Apparently righteous anger wasn't enough to quench the desire he felt for her.

"You should have told me you were coming," she blurted out, crossing her arms over her chest. The edges of her sweater slid back and the rounded bump of her belly was proudly displayed.

Under that steady regard, Aine pulled her sweater over in front of her, disguising the bump.

Anger, betrayal and a whisper of panic rose up inside him and settled in his chest. "I should have told you?" he asked. "Why? So you could be gone when I got here?"

"No," she said, lifting that stubborn chin of hers even higher. "This is my home, I wouldn't have gone, but I might have been prepared—"

"For more lies?" he interrupted.

"I didn't lie to you," she insisted, chin high, eyes flashing. "Exactly."

"Really?" He walked closer and closer until he was just a breath away from her and she was forced to tip her head back to meet his eyes. God, her scent wrapped itself around him and snaked into his brain, where it tangled with memories and lies and secrets and drove him even closer to the edge. "You didn't lie. When I asked if you were pregnant, what did you say?"

"That you'd nothing to worry about," she snapped, pushing away from him. "'Tis no more than the truth. My child is not yours to worry over."

"My child, too, Aine." God, just saying those words out loud gave Brady a jolt that shook him right to the bones.

"You don't want him. I do."

"Him?" Brady asked.

She sighed and her shoulders slumped. "Aye. 'Tis a boy."

A son. He had a son. Hard to wrap his brain around, but knowing what the baby was made this so much more real. More immediate. "And he's healthy?"

"He is," she said, laying one hand protectively over her belly.

He caught the action and his heart gave a hard thump. She'd been pregnant for five months. She'd been here, building a life without him. Planning a future for their child without him. He hadn't suspected. Hadn't sensed anything during all of the conversations he'd had with her. It seemed he should have known somehow. The fact that he hadn't was due to her.

"I had a right to know, Aine."

"You would only have offered me money—"

Stung, mostly because she was probably right, he said, "You don't know that."

"Don't I? When you were in such a rush to get rid of *me*, your first thought was to offer me a raise."

He ground his teeth together in pure frustration. Yes, she had a point, but that didn't negate the fact that she was in the wrong here and had no excuse good enough for what she'd done.

The thought of being a father had never really entered his mind. It wasn't as if he had any notion how to be a part of a family. But now that he was faced with the very real existence of a child he'd created, he could admit to himself that it wasn't only worry and anger charging through his system.

For the first time in his life, he would be a part of something. His child. And he wouldn't let anyone cut him out of the boy's life.

"You made yourself clear in California, Brady," Aine was saying. "You wanted no more from me, so why would I assume you would want my child?"

"Half yours," he corrected. "Half mine."

"Well, short of Solomon's solution to this situation, I don't know what you want of me."

"I want to know my kid," he snapped. "And I want him to know me. I won't have my son wondering where his parents are. Wondering why he wasn't good enough for his father to stick around or why—"

He broke off, appalled at the words rushing from him. He hadn't talked about his childhood to anyone. Not even the Ryan brothers knew the whole story, and damned if Brady was going to spill his guts to the woman who'd lied to him. The woman who stood there looking at him through green eyes shining now with anxiety and curiosity.

"Why would he think that?" she asked quietly.

"He won't. He'll never have to," Brady assured her, moving in close again. "We've got a lot of talking to do."

"I suppose we do, at that." She sighed and walked to one corner of the room. "I've a tea set up here. Would you like a cup?"

"Are we going to be civilized now?" he asked wryly.

She glanced at him. "We can certainly try."

"Right." Nodding, he walked along behind her and tried to let go of the hard knot of anger in his guts. Wouldn't do him any good to stay angry. Aine would just have to learn that he wasn't going anywhere. Not until they figured out what to do from here.

"The tea services will be in every room," she was saying, plugging in a kettle and readying two cups. "It's not proper tea, of course, but bags. Still, it's welcome on a cold summer day."

"Cold summer day," he mused, stuffing his hands into his pockets as he followed after her. "Don't hear that much at home."

"True enough, but Ireland's a different matter, isn't it?" She busied herself with the tea bags and cups, and when the water in the kettle boiled, she poured it. "The kitchen's not ready for use as yet, with the stove not installed." She was talking faster, showing nerves she otherwise would have hidden. "I've been eating sandwiches mostly, since the fridge is working fine, or eating with Mum and Robbie. If you're planning on staying a bit—"

"I am," he assured her.

She nodded. "Then, sandwiches for you as well, or there's the village where you can find pub grub."

"Sounds delicious." He leaned one shoulder against the wall and watched as she finished preparing the tea and handed him a cup.

"'Tis good," she told him. "Mick Hannigan's wife has a way with shepherd's pie."

"I'll keep it in mind," he said and couldn't care less about the pub, the village or pretty much anything else but the woman in front of him and the child nestled inside her. To keep her off balance, he asked, "How's the work on the castle coming?

She gave him a curious glance. "As I've told you every week. Much progress has been made, though we've hit a bump or two along the way."

"What kind of bumps?" he asked.

"No more than you'd expect on such a big job," she said. "We've had some trouble with supplies arriving or being misordered, but we're dealing with them."

He frowned into his cup. "You didn't say anything to me about this."

"What would you do about it from California?" She threw that question over her shoulder as she walked to one of the chairs in front of the hearth and sat down.

"I can make phone calls," he told her as he took the chair beside her.

"As can I," she pointed out. "And have, as it's my job, isn't it? The only real worry now is the slate tiles for the roof. They've been delayed again, and should a storm hit—"

"I'll talk to the supplier tomorrow."

"I don't need your help to do my job any more than I need your help to care for my child," she said.

"For the baby, you can't know yet what you'll need," he countered. "About the roof tiles, it's my castle. I'll call and get the damn things here."

"Because you're a man, of course."

He grinned. "We use what we have."

"And you'll offer them money, as well?"

"Someday," Brady mused, "you're going to have to explain to me just what it is you've got against money."

She sniffed, took a sip of tea and laid her head against the chair back. "You being here will only make things harder, Brady." Her voice was so soft, he nearly missed her words. "Take one of the rooms on this floor, spend the night, check out the castle to your heart's content." She turned her head to spear him with a forest green glance. "Then, for both our sakes, go home."

Well, now he had an idea of how she'd felt when he'd practically pushed her onto a plane for Ireland. The difference between them was he had no intention of leaving.

Brady took a sip of the tea and wished it was coffee. Or better yet, Irish whiskey. Then he met her eyes in a steady stare and vowed, "I'll take a room, Aine. But I'm not going anywhere. Get used to it."

Nine

The next morning, Aine was up and out of the castle early. Yes, it was cowardly to slip away just to avoid Brady, but she simply couldn't deal with another "discussion" about the baby. She knew going to see her mother wouldn't prevent the next confrontation—only delay it. But in the meantime, she needed the space to think.

"He's angry," Aine said over a cup of tea at her mother's kitchen table.

"Of course he is," Molly told her daughter. "The man's just found out he's to be a father. And that you kept the news from him." She smoothed one hand over Aine's hair. "You should have told him, love. He had the right to know."

"Maybe," Aine admitted, remembering the look on Brady's face yesterday when he'd spotted the evidence of her pregnancy.

Molly pushed a plate of sugar biscuits toward her

daughter. "Have one to tide you over until I make break-fast."

Aine was almost too tired to chew the cookie. She hadn't slept all night. How could she, with Brady just down the hall from her? Missing him had been hard on her when an ocean separated them. It was impossible with only twenty feet between them. Because he was here, in Ireland, and still not hers.

Seeing him again after five long months had nearly torn her in two. Her head warred with her heart and too often came out the loser. Even knowing there was no future for her with Brady, she couldn't stop the yearning.

"What am I to do, Mum?"

Molly reached across the table and patted her daughter's hand. "Follow your heart, always, Aine. You can't make a mistake if you do."

Wryly, Aine smoothed her palm over her belly. "I followed my heart five months ago…"

"You did." Molly's blue eyes were kind and full of understanding. "And if you keep doing just that, you'll perhaps come out the other side with your heart whole and a future to look forward to."

Not once had her mother been anything but supportive in the past five months. Aine knew just how lucky she was in that. Molly was on her side, no matter what. Robbie, on the other hand, had been furious as only a younger brother could be when he felt his sister had been used and discarded. Molly, though, had been steadfast without even a flicker of disappointment in her only daughter.

Aine loved her mother, but Molly was a hopeless romantic. Aine knew the truth. That Brady would never be in a relationship with her. The manager of his hotel?

No…wealthy men didn't marry women like her. What drove him now were duty and his own sense of honor.

"I don't like that look in your eye, Aine," her mother said.

"Sorry, but you don't know him, Mum." Frowning into her tea, she said, "He'll see the baby—and me, for that matter—as a burden to be carried. A debt to be settled. There's no thought of more from him because he doesn't *want* more."

"Duty's not so far from love," Molly said. "A man feels a responsibility to his child, to the family he's made…"

"We're not a family," Aine interrupted.

"I'm not finished. Duty may drive his actions, but if he felt no duty to the child he made, you wouldn't want him anyway, would you?"

"I suppose not," Aine admitted, and acknowledged silently that she hadn't thought of it like that before. Brady wanting to do the right thing was the mark of a good man. If he didn't care on some level, he'd have left the moment he saw her rounded belly.

"Still, he didn't want me before," Aine admitted, turning her cup between her hands, watching the tea inside slosh against the sides. "He couldn't put me on a plane fast enough the moment we got…close."

"Yet he's here, in Ireland," her mother pointed out.

Shaking her head, Aine said, "He came to check on the castle."

Molly snorted and gave her daughter's hand a hard pat. "Did he? And in all these months, he's never once done that. He bought the castle without seeing it. Began costly renovations without seeing it. Why is it *now*, I wonder, the man's here?"

Hope was a dangerous thing, and even knowing that,

Aine couldn't keep a tiny blossom of it from forming inside her. But if she held to hope, wouldn't she just be crushed all the more when that hope dissolved?

"Do you love him?" Molly asked gently.

Aine had asked herself that question many times over the past several months and the truth was, she'd even tried to talk herself out of what she felt for Brady Finn. But the fact remained. "Fool that I am, yes. I do."

"Love makes fools of all of us," Molly assured her. "And if you love the man, you can't give up on him."

When her mother stood up and moved to the stove, Aine watched her. Molly wore black slacks and a deep green sweater, and her thick auburn hair, now streaked with silver threads, curled under at chin level. Molly tucked her hair behind her ears and reached for a skillet to start breakfast. Turning the fire on under the pan, she moved off to get the fixings from the fridge, which was currently hiccupping noisily in the corner.

Aine sighed and glanced around the familiar kitchen with its white walls, red cabinets and aging appliances. It was neat and clean as a church, but like the castle itself, the guest cottage was in sore need of repair. She'd like to have the cottage renovated at the same time as the castle, but how, she couldn't imagine.

Making the castle over was one thing, but to fix up the cottage where her family lived was something else again. Then she wondered if Brady would continue to allow her family to live on the grounds. What if he didn't? Worry spread in the pit of her stomach like an ink spill, dark and thick. If he chose to rent out the cottage to guests as well, where would her family go? Her mother couldn't afford a higher rent, and with the baby coming, Aine wouldn't be able to help much.

Her head was swimming with this whole new set of worries when she heard a knock on the door.

"Now, who in the world?" her mother asked no one in particular as she left the kitchen to answer the summons.

Aine took another sugar biscuit and had a big bite when she heard the rumble of voices and recognized Brady's. She pushed to her feet, hurried into the main room and saw him step inside, taking her mother's hand.

"Mrs. Donovan, I'm Brady Finn, the father of your grandson."

His dark hair tumbled over his forehead and he wore a black leather jacket over a dark red T-shirt and black jeans. His boots were scuffed and appeared well used. He looked impossibly gorgeous, and when Aine felt a stir inside her she nearly sighed. There was just no getting past what she felt for the man, even knowing she *should*.

Molly threw her daughter a quick glance before shifting her gaze back to Brady with a smile. "Aren't you a handsome one? It's good you've come."

"Well," Brady said, "when I couldn't find Aine at the castle, I remembered she said her family lived in the cottage. I hoped I'd find her here."

"And so she is." Molly tugged him into the house. "Come in, won't you?"

"Why are you here?" Aine asked.

"To meet your family."

He said it as though she should have expected him, which she hadn't. As he'd told her many times, Brady Finn didn't do families.

"I was just making breakfast," Molly said into the silence. "You'll join us."

"Thank you." Brady threw a half smile at Aine over

his shoulder as Molly tugged him in her wake toward the kitchen.

When Aine followed after them, she found Brady already seated at the table and her mother dropping sausages and bacon into a pan to sizzle.

"That smells great," Brady said, fixing his gaze on Aine as she moved farther into the room.

"You'll have tea, as well," Molly told him, then fired a look at her daughter. "Aine, fetch another cup and pour some tea for the man."

Aine caught the gleam of amusement in Brady's dark blue eyes. As she poured tea and then automatically refilled the kettle and set it on to boil again, she asked herself why he was doing all of this. Duty was one thing, but when a woman told a man she didn't want or need his guilt money, why would he stay? Introduce himself to her family? Lay claim to her child?

The luscious scent of frying bacon and sausage sizzled into the air as Molly efficiently cracked eggs into a bowl and whipped them into a froth.

"How long have you lived here, Mrs. Donovan?" he asked.

"Oh, call me Molly, love, as we're in the way of being family now, aren't we?"

He grinned again, and Aine wondered if her mother was doing this on purpose. "He's not family, Mum."

"If he's not, I don't know who is," her mother countered. "Now, then, Brady, the Donovans have lived here five years now, since we lost Aine's father to a storm at sea."

He sipped at his tea, then gave her a solemn nod. "Aine told me. I was sorry to hear it."

"Thank you." Molly gave him a smile that took the

edge off the sheen of tears clouding her bright blue eyes at the mention of the man she still loved and missed. "The cottage was a godsend to us, for sure, as Robbie was so young and Aine was working here at the castle…"

Aine watched Brady as her mother continued to talk, regaling him with family stories while she cooked. And Brady took it all in, looking as comfortable in the shabby kitchen as he had in the plush penthouse that was his home. Anyone looking at him would never think him a billionaire.

Then he smiled at her and her heart turned over in her chest. She'd missed him, damn the man. She hadn't wanted to, but it was hard not to think of the man who had given her a baby. And it was more than that, as well. She'd missed the contradiction and contrariness of the man. She'd missed looking at him and feeling that slow spin of something lovely sliding through her. And she knew that when he left again, the pain of missing him would be even sharper than it had been before.

But of course he had to leave. The fact that she loved him changed nothing. There was nothing between them but a child each of them wanted. He wouldn't stay, so why was he here, charming her mother?

"Is he the one?" Robbie's voice shook her out of her daydream.

Aine stepped to her younger brother and put one hand on his arm. It still amazed her that at almost eighteen, Robbie towered over her. Tall and lanky like their father had been, Robbie's gaze was locked on Brady, and he didn't look willing to be charmed.

Brady stood up and held out one hand to the boy. "Brady Finn. You're Robbie."

"I am," the boy said, whipping his hair back from his face as he took Brady's hand in a hard grip.

The room went quiet as Aine and her mother watched, neither of them knowing quite what to expect. There was a long moment where the two of them stared hard into each other's eyes and seemed to be each taking the measure of the other. Finally, though, Robbie asked, "You've come to see Aine. Why?"

"Robbie…"

"'Tis a question I'd like answered, too," Molly said, ignoring her daughter's sigh.

Brady let go of Robbie's hand and looked the boy square in the eyes, giving him the respect of treating him like an equal. "I didn't know about the baby," he said quietly, "or I would have been here sooner."

Aine felt a twinge of shame that she'd lied to the man, but it was too late to change that now.

Robbie only nodded and waited for Brady to continue.

"I've been doing a lot of thinking since I found out about the baby," he said, looking from one to the other of them. "And I think I've got the solution. Aine and I will get married."

"Wonderful!" from Molly.

"Good," from Robbie.

"We will not," from Aine.

Brady wasn't surprised. He'd known what her reaction would be, and how could he blame her? Not as if he was husband and father material after all. No one knew that better than he did. But all through the long night, he'd considered and rejected dozens of possibilities.

She wouldn't take his money. She'd made that plain enough, and he wasn't about to let her and his son go without whatever they needed. In his whole life, he'd never had anyone rely on him. He'd been alone and he'd liked it that way. Until Aine. After she'd left, the solitude he had always prized hadn't seemed as comfortable as it had before.

He'd missed her laughter, the way her eyes narrowed and her chin lifted when she was ready to argue with him. He'd missed the feel of her, the taste of her. And he hadn't been able to find any damn peace without her.

Now there was a child who was only alive because of him, and he wouldn't fail that boy. The one thing Brady could do for his son was to marry his mother and ensure that the two of them had whatever they needed.

"He's not serious," Aine said, shaking her head.

Brady shifted his gaze to hers, willing her to see in his eyes that he'd never meant anything more.

"He looks as though he is." Molly waved them all into chairs at the table, then brought platters of food and set them down. "Everyone tuck in while it's hot, now."

Brady settled in to eat breakfast with Aine's family and didn't look her way again. He knew what she must be thinking, because he wasn't far from thinking the same thing himself. *Married?* He'd never thought to marry anyone. But times and situations changed, he reminded himself as he took another bite of scrambled eggs.

All night, his mind had raged, going from one possibility to another, and finally he'd even called Mike Ryan to tell him what was going on. While Robbie talked eagerly of zombies and programming and his mother watched him proudly, Brady's mind drifted back to that conversation.

"She's pregnant?"

"Yeah." Brady paced his room, pausing now and

again to stare out the windows at the night beyond the glass. "She says she doesn't want anything from me. Doesn't need me." And wasn't that a kick in the gut?

"And you believe that?"

Brady stopped, frowned and thought about it. No one had ever needed him before, so why would Aine? "I've no reason not to."

"You have every reason not to. She's giving you an out, that's all." Mike sighed and then patiently spoke again. "You told her you weren't interested in a relationship and sent her back home, right?"

"Yeah..." Brady scrubbed one hand over his face at the memory, wishing he could wipe it away.

"So why would she think you'd changed your mind now? She's just saying what she thinks you want to hear, that's all."

"You think?"

"Please." Mike snorted. "The question is, what are you going to do about this? Give her what she thinks she wants, or what she needs?"

Brady looked at Aine and something inside him tightened uncomfortably. Her eyes were hypnotic as they latched on to his, and he felt himself wishing that things were different. That he was a different man. But he didn't belong in this cozy family setting, and he knew it. The best he could do was provide for Aine and their child whether she liked it or not.

"Did you really think I'd agree to marry you when you've made it clear time and again you've no wish for a relationship at all?"

Hadn't taken her long to fight back, Brady thought.

They'd hardly taken more than ten steps from the cottage when she turned on him.

"You will marry me. If not for you, then for our son," Brady said, taking her arm and steering her toward the castle.

"No, I won't," she argued, whipping her auburn hair back from her face when the wind tossed it into a tangle. "I'll not live a lie. Why does this matter to you? In California you made it plain you weren't interested in becoming involved with your hotel manager."

"What?" Brady shook his head and stared at her. "That had nothing to do with anything."

"Oh, aye, it does. You're a rich man. I wouldn't know how to live in your world, and you've no clue about mine." She tugged her arm free of him and started walking faster. "Our son will be just fine without his parents being married."

"No, he won't." Brady pulled her to a stop beneath one of the oak trees and whirled her around until her back was to the gnarled trunk. Dappled shade danced across her features and shone in the eyes that were narrowed on him. "You think times have changed. It's no big deal for a kid to have no father. Well, they haven't changed that much. And my kid's not going to suffer because his parents couldn't get along."

"And marriage between two people who don't want it is better?" she asked.

"We don't have to live together." He braced his hands on either side of her head and leaned in. He'd thought this through and knew this was the answer. "We'll be married and stay married until after our child is born."

"And then what? A divorce?" Shaking her head, she said, "This must be the first proposal in history that comes with a plan for ending the marriage before it begins. You want to marry me, just not live with me, is that it?"

"I want my son to know that his parents were married."

"However briefly, then?"

"Look I'm no good at the day-to-day relationship thing, but that's my son you're carrying, and he's going to know that I cared enough about him to marry his mother."

"How do you know you're no good at it?" she asked.

"You can't live what you don't know. Anyway, that's the deal," he said shortly, stuffing both hands into his pockets.

"Well, isn't that the most romantic thing I've ever heard."

He stalked away from her and then back again, demanding, "Who's talking about romance?"

This wasn't about love and happily-ever-after, Brady told himself. This was about making sure she and their baby were safe. His son would have his name, and even if he and Aine didn't live together, the child would know his father cared.

"Not you," she said flatly.

"Aine, let me do this. For you. For our baby." He'd never asked anyone for anything before, and the words didn't come easily. "It's important to me that you and our son be safe."

"Of course he'll be safe. Brady…" She reached up to cup his cheek, and her touch was so warm, so tender, it shook him right down to the soles of his feet. "What drives you so? What keeps you from wanting to be a part of something? What makes you propose with the promise of an ending rather than a beginning?"

He stepped back because having her touch him was both a blessing and a curse. He couldn't think with her hand on him. Could hardly breathe without her touch. Staring into green eyes looking up at him anxiously, he felt himself bend. Felt himself need, and he fought it back.

There was nothing he wanted more than to pick her up, carry her into the castle and stretch her out on a bed. He wanted his hands on her, wanted to explore her new curves, caress the mound of his child and hold her tightly enough that the ache inside him eased.

But if he was with her again, he'd never let her go. He knew that now, and he *had* to let her go. For everyone's sake. So Brady pushed his own wants aside, burying them beneath the layers of secrets he was already hoarding. And he tried to make her understand.

"Your family's great," he said with a quick look at the cottage. "You grew up with that, so you know how to create it on your own. I don't. And so I don't try because I won't risk failing."

"You're talking in riddles. Tell me what it is that's tearing at you."

He shook his head. "You wouldn't understand."

Brady's campaign to win Aine over was relentless.

For the next few days, everywhere she turned, there he was. He kept his hand at her back when they walked together, made sure she sat down and put her feet up in the afternoon and helped her with the castle's books.

He had tea with her every afternoon, and in the evenings, he insisted on being with her, tempting her too much with the needs and wishes that clamored in her heart. Aine felt as though she was under siege by a gentle warrior determined to win the war with stubborn, relentless attention.

Her body was on fire and there was no relief in sight. He didn't try to make love to her again, and Aine wanted him more every day. Was he intentionally *punishing* her—and himself—for her turning down his plan of marriage and divorce? But what kind of thing was that for a man to offer? Did he not see that by giving her the vow to end the marriage, he was also giving her a reason to never accept the marriage? How could she when she knew the man was only biding his time before he disappeared from her life again?

He went into the village with her to run errands, and everywhere they went, he introduced himself as her fiancé and invited all of the villagers to a wedding that wasn't going to happen. He took over most of her jobs, seeing to the supplies being ordered, the work being done, and even had the makers of the roof tiles complying and promising delivery within the week—which was just infuriating.

He spent time with Robbie, showing the boy the ins and outs of building a video game from the ground up. Then he would spend hours with the boy, playing "Fate Castle" on Robbie's old television.

Molly couldn't say enough about Brady, who fixed a leaky pipe for her, then repaired a broken cabinet hinge. He was winning over her family, her friends—even the workmen at the castle sang his praises.

And every day, Brady proposed to Aine again, leaving her shaken and wishing that he actually loved her and really meant to live with her and make that family she wanted so badly. But she knew it was a lie. She knew it was only his sense of duty that kept him there and her heart hurt with the knowledge.

Even Brian, her accountant, had promised her forever until she'd ended their engagement. And now the man she truly loved body and soul promised her a beginning and an ending in the same proposal.

She buried the longing, the misery, in working on the hotel's books and planning for the grand reopening. In her office off the main lobby, Aine studied the computer screen and tried to push thoughts of Brady out of her mind. She emailed their website manager and arranged for him to send out email announcements about the changes happening at Castle Butler.

Then they set up a plan to run a web contest, with the grand prize being an all-expenses-paid one-week stay at Fate Castle. Brady and the Ryans had already agreed to it, and Aine thought it was a wonderful way to generate interest in the new hotel.

While the sound of work went on around her, Aine buried her personal miseries in her job, and after a couple of hours thought she was feeling better. All she had to do was stand strong against Brady's ridiculous notion of being married only to divorce. Soon enough, he'd tire of the challenge of wearing her down and go back to his life, allowing her to return to her own.

Without him.

Oh, the thought of that made her ache to her soul. Being with him again was so hard, knowing that she would lose him a second—and no doubt *last*—time.

When her phone rang, she grabbed it up, grateful to be drawn out of her own thoughts. "Hello?"

"Aine, come to the cottage," her mother said, voice breathless. "You must see this!"

Before Aine could ask what was wrong, what was happening, Molly hung up. Aine was out the door a moment later, hurrying across the grounds to the guest cottage.

There were three men on the cottage roof, replacing old, worn shingles with new. There were four more men on the outside of the stone cottage, who were busily painting the stones a soft cream color. What was going on?

Her mother met her on the front steps and waved excitedly. "Come in, come in!" She took Aine's hand when she was close enough and dragged her into the cottage. "Isn't it wonderful? Brady said I wasn't to worry about a leaking roof anymore and before I knew it, he had men on the roof fixing the whole thing. And painters, as well. Isn't it a lovely color?"

Molly's cheeks were flushed and a wide grin split her face and danced in her eyes as she handed Aine a manila envelope. "And then this happened!"

Aine opened it, pulled out a sheaf of papers and skimmed them. Then she read it all again, more slowly, then checked the back page and saw Brady's signature. She lifted her gaze to her mother's. "He's signed over the cottage to you."

Tears pooled in Molly's eyes, spilled over and were wiped away again. "He's a darling man, Aine. The note he sent with the papers said he wanted us to have the home we love. Isn't he a darling man?"

"Darling," Aine whispered, stunned nearly speechless. She couldn't believe he'd done something so kind for her mother. Now Molly would never again worry about making a rent payment, and the small house she'd called home for years was really hers.

"I was never so surprised. I had palpitations when I looked at those papers, I can tell you. But the dear man wasn't finished." She tugged her daughter back to the kitchen. "Look, will you just look at this!"

There was a shiny new cherry-red Aga stove installed in the space where Molly's ancient cooker had been only that morning. And in the corner stood a cherry-red refrigerator, shining and new and making hardly a sound louder than a purr of perfection.

"Isn't it grand?" Molly ran one hand across the stove top, then tsked at the fingerprints left behind. Quickly, she grabbed a cloth and rubbed the surface shiny again. "I've never in my life had such a stove as this. And the refrigerator, Aine! So big, so quiet…" She sighed happily. "And he bought them in red, the dear man, as he must have noticed how I love the color."

Clutching her dish towel in one hand, Molly plopped down onto a kitchen chair and looked around her in astonishment. "It's too much by far, but to know that our home is now really *ours*… Well, it's a gift beyond price is what it is."

Aine couldn't speak. All she could do was watch her mother's excited features as she sighed happily over what had happened. Brady had done this without a word to Aine. He'd seen the shape of things in the cottage and had gone out of his way to fix them. A new roof, fresh paint and then this—he'd transformed the heart of Molly's home. And buying *red*, of all things. He'd noticed the red cabinets in the kitchen and had guessed, rightly, that her mother would love the bright and shiny color.

But far more than that, he'd given her mother *security*. A life without worry. Aine's heart gave a twist and she felt the sting of tears burn her eyes.

"And that's not all." Molly pushed out of the chair as if she couldn't sit still. "He's sent a grand new television for Robbie and a new game machine, as well. Oh, and something he said is an art program that all young designers should have. When the boy gets home from school, he'll be beside himself."

"Why?" Aine whispered. "Why is he doing this?"

"Darling, can't you see why?" Molly cupped Aine's face in her palms and said, "He loves you, darling girl. He's no idea what to do about it, though, so he does this instead. He's showing you without words what you mean to him."

Aine would like nothing more than to believe that, but how could she? He'd sent her away, hadn't he? He'd as much as told her he wasn't interested. He'd proposed, but had also planned a divorce. Did a man in love do that?

"You're wrong, Mum," she finally said sadly. "It's only that he's a rich man, and when he finds a problem, it's his way to throw money at it."

"He didn't need to throw it at *us*," her mother said. "He did all of this for *you*."

Was her mother right? Did Brady love her? And if he did, why wouldn't he tell her? It was time, Aine told herself, to get some answers.

Ten

She found Brady in the back of the castle, near the maze. He turned when she came toward him and asked, "Do we really need this maze? Takes up a lot of room and—"

Aine walked right up to him, cupped his face in her palms and went up on her toes to kiss him. The taste of him after so long was soul stirring. Here was what she wanted, needed. Here was love so rich and thick it filled her, body and soul.

She felt his surprise, then his surrender as he fisted his hands at her back and pulled her in tight and close. Pressed against him, she felt the solid thump of his heartbeat, felt the hard strength of him, and knew she didn't want to live the rest of her life without him.

He deepened the kiss and Aine parted her lips for his tongue to sweep along hers, stealing her breath, making her heartbeat gallop and her knees weak. Brady Finn was in her heart and mind, and she needed him to know that. A cold wind whipped around them, binding them closer as watery sunlight filtered through clouds thick and gray. She let go of everything but the moment and gave herself up to the rush of emotions crowding through her.

When he finally raised his head and looked down at her, he gave her a half smile. "What was that for?"

"I've been talking with my mother."

"Ah…" His eyes cooled, and a wall she was too familiar with came up between them, effectively shutting her out. He stepped back, leaving her feeling alone, adrift. Turning to look at the maze again, he said only, "Well, you're welcome."

She wouldn't let either of them back away this time, though. This was too important. Too *real* not to acknowledge. Aine was determined to tell him how she felt and *demand* that he admit the same.

"That kiss wasn't only a thank-you," she said softly, walking around until she stood in front of him again and he was forced to look at her. He needed to know the whole truth and it was long past time she allowed herself to say the three words that meant everything. "It was also an 'I love you.'"

She saw his eyes flash then darken and go cool again, all in the span of a single heartbeat. His features went hard and detached, so she tried again. "Brady. I said I love you."

"I heard you." He stepped around her, again focusing on the bloody maze that Aine couldn't care about at the moment. "But you don't mean it. You're grateful, that's all. Now about the maze…"

"Devil take the blasted maze," she muttered. "And don't tell me what I feel or I don't. 'Tis insulting."

"Then, don't confuse love with gratitude," he snapped, sparing her only a quick look before focusing on the maze again. "If we tore this down…"

She huffed out a furious breath and said, "We'll not tear the maze down." Irritated that the first time she told him she loved him, he couldn't be bothered to believe her. And it was clear he wouldn't listen to her until they'd gotten the maze issue dealt with. "It was laid out by Lord Butler's great-granddaughter in 1565. 'Tis as much a part of the castle as the stone walls and battlements. All it needs is a bit of tending." She shot the raggedy bushes a hard look. "A good gardener will have it looking as it should in no time. Then maybe your gamer people can hunt werewolves in it." She waved a negligent hand. "Or we'll have prizes in the center of the maze for those who find their way in and out again."

"Hmm…not a bad idea," he said, and walked into the maze, quickly disappearing behind the high thick box-wood hedges.

Aine swallowed the bubble of temper threatening to spew and ruin the lovely romantic moment she'd planned. Why was the man so resolved to ignore what she was trying to tell him? With pride pushing her on and love clawing at her heart, she went after him, and when she caught up, she took a grip on his forearm and turned him to her. "You tell me why you don't believe I love you."

He looked at her and his eyes were as dark as the clouds rushing in from the sea. The wind sharpened, and even with the protection of the hedges surrounding them, she felt the chill it brought. But the cold she saw in his eyes went deeper than a harsh sea gust. Worry curled in the pit of her stomach, but she stood her ground, refusing to let him walk away this time. Seconds fell into minutes and those, too, crawled past as she waited. Just when she thought he would never answer her, he did.

"Because no one ever has," he muttered thickly before scrubbing one hand across his mouth as if he could wipe away the taste of the words.

She'd no idea what to make of that, but Aine could see what the words had cost him. Then he laughed shortly, and she winced at the pain in the sound of it.

"Brady," she said, sliding her hand along his forearm in a gesture meant to be comforting. "Talk to me. Tell me what it is that haunts you so."

He looked down at her hand, then lifted his gaze to hers. When he started speaking, his voice was low and strained. "You're always saying we're too different. Well, you're right, but not for the reasons you think." He moved in on her, backed her up against the maze hedge and loomed over her, his gaze sweeping her features as if carving them into his memory. "You want to know why I won't stay married and build a family? Because I've never had one. Never known one." He took a breath and released it. "When I was six years old, my mother dumped me on the state and left. Never saw her again." Old anger, old pain, glittered in his eyes like dark water in moonlight. "Who the hell knows who my father was? I went into the system. They shuttled me from home to home, with me carting my stuff around in paper sacks like trash." He eased back from her, putting at least a few inches between them. Almost as if he couldn't bear to be close to her when reliving his past.

Aine didn't know what to say, how to help, so she stayed quiet and listened, her heart breaking.

"From six to thirteen, I was in five different foster homes. None of 'em worked. None of 'em wanted me to stay." He swallowed hard. "After that, I didn't try any-more. Just lived at the home, went to school and bided my time until I could get out on my own."

"Brady, I'm so sorry..." She reached for him, but he twisted away and her hand fell helplessly to her side.

"I'm not telling you for your pity," he ground out. "Hell, I've never told anyone all of this, not even the Ryans. They know some, not all. But you need to know. You need to understand. You think I'm rich? All I've got is money. You're way richer than I am in every possible way, Aine." He pushed one hand through his hair, took a deep breath and blurted out, "You grew up with Molly, your father, your brother. You had a place. You had... love. You never doubted it—why would you? It was al-ways there." He shoved his hands into his jacket pock-ets as if he couldn't figure out what to do with them. "I don't know what that's like. Wouldn't know the first thing about being a part of it. So yeah, you're richer than I'll ever be, and damned if I don't envy you for it."

Aine's heart ached for the boy he had been. But... for the man he was, she felt nothing but exasperation. Couldn't he see that he was so much more than he be-lieved himself to be? He hadn't grown up with love, as she had. But there was so much love locked away inside him, burning to get out. She saw it in his friendship with the Ryans. With his generosity to her mother and brother. And she felt it in every touch he'd ever given her.

"I don't do families because I don't know how," he admitted and speared her gaze with his. "And if I tried and failed, that would damage my own kid, and I won't risk that."

Maybe the two of them weren't as different as she'd thought they were. Money, after all, was cold comfort if you had no one to share it with. He thought his worth was measured only by his bank account. That was why, she told herself, he was always offering her money. Because somewhere inside him he couldn't believe that she wanted him for himself.

"The only way you can damage a child is by not loving it," she said softly. "By not being there."

"It's not the only way, Aine," he said tightly. His gaze slipped down to the curve of her belly, then lifted to meet her eyes. "I don't know anything about families, Aine. They are not for me."

"You're the most stubborn of men," she snapped. "And blind, as well."

"What?"

"You do have a family, Brady. The Ryan brothers are your family whether you see it or not, and you do just fine there, don't you?" She moved in closer. "And you've claimed Mum's and Robbie's hearts, as well. You've made a place for yourself with them in such a short time." Tipping her head back, she stared directly into his eyes so there could be no misunderstanding when she said, "And you've mine, Brady. You have my heart."

He shook his head. "You didn't hear a word I said, did you?"

"I heard everything." Aine grabbed his hand and held it to her belly. At their joined touch, the baby kicked as if he knew his father was there within reach. She watched Brady's eyes widen with awe and felt her heart turn over again. How this man touched her. How he moved her. How he infuriated her. "Don't you see, Brady? You've made a family already. You've got me now, and the baby. Our son."

He stroked her belly, bent his head and kissed her, gently, tenderly, his teeth nibbling at her bottom lip and making her insides go soft and yielding. When he broke the kiss, he rested his forehead against hers and whispered, "You say you love me, Aine."

"I do."

"Then, marry me."

"If you stay," she promised.

"I can't," he said. "I can't take the chance of messing up yours and my kid's life. I don't know how to be what you want me to be."

"You *won't*, you mean." Frustration, anger and love circled around inside her, battering at her heart and soul. Every cell in her body cried out for what she couldn't have, and she heard herself say, "So once again, you'll sacrifice what you want for my own good. You'll turn away from what could be and cling to a past that brings you nothing but pain."

"Don't you get it?" His voice was as hard as stone, as merciless as the expression on his face. "I can't have what I want without risking ruining it. I won't do that to you—or the baby."

Hurt and feeling rejected once again by the man she loved and wanted more than anything, Aine moved away from him, though it tore her in two to do it. Until he realized what he had, what *they* could have, all of the words in the world wouldn't make a difference.

Meeting his gaze, she said, "You know what the hardest part of all this is? Mum was right. You *do* love me. You've said it in every way but words. And I'll not accept less from you, Brady. I deserve all. We deserve all. I want the words and the promise of them. When you find them within yourself, I'll be here."

* * *

By morning he was gone.

Two days later he was alone in his office, watching the sunrise. He hadn't been able to sleep since leaving Ireland, so there was no point staying in bed pretending otherwise. He took a sip of coffee and spun around in his desk chair to look out the windows.

The view didn't ease him because he hardly saw it. Instead, his mind dredged up images of Ireland and the castle…and Aine.

Brady didn't see her before he left. Better that way, he assured himself. Easier.

On who? a voice in his mind asked. *Her? Or you?*

The answer was both, of course. He wasn't a coward, ducking out without seeing her for fear he'd change his mind. He was doing the right thing here. Making the hard choice for all of them. Molly understood. He'd stopped at the cottage to see her on his way out, and rather than being angry that he was leaving, she'd hugged him and told him to come back soon. That he'd always be welcome.

He didn't think Aine felt the same way, but he couldn't really blame her for that.

She loved him.

Pain exploded in his chest and radiated throughout his body. Never in his life had anyone ever loved him, and he'd walked away from it. From her.

He couldn't breathe.

Just like he hadn't been able to sleep in his penthouse suite. It had been too…empty. Too sterile.

He had the distinct feeling his whole damn life was going to be empty from here on out. Brady rubbed the center of his chest, hoping to ease the hollowed-out sensation that had been with him since he'd left Ireland. As if his heart had been carved out and the echoing cavern it left behind was filled with ice.

"What're you doing here so early?" Mike spoke up from the open doorway.

"Couldn't sleep." He took another long drink of coffee, hoping to hell caffeine would kick in soon.

"Wonder why." Mike strolled into the office, dropped into a chair opposite Brady's desk and settled in.

"Jet lag." Brady frowned at his friend. He wasn't in the mood for conversation. Hell, he wasn't in the mood for anything.

"Yeah, I don't think so." Mike folded his hands over his abdomen, tipped his head to one side and said, "You want to tell me why you left Ireland in such a damn hurry? When you had a woman like Aine there? And a son on the way?"

He never should have called Mike when he'd first found out about the baby. If he hadn't, then his misery would be private.

"I had to." Brady set his coffee aside, pushed up from his chair and walked to the window. Leaning one shoulder on the wall, he stared blindly out the glass. "She says she loves me."

"A beautiful woman, pregnant with your kid, tells you she loves you. Of *course* you had to leave!" Astonishment colored Mike's voice. "Are you an idiot?"

"No, I'm not. I just know that I don't belong there." Brady spun around and glared at his friend. "How the hell could I be with her and my kid, Mike? I don't know how to do the family thing." God, he was tired of explaining that. Tired of hearing that his past was going to reach out and strangle his future. But facts were facts. "You can't do something you've never done."

"You are nuts. Because what you just said is bull." Mike stood up, planted both hands on Brady's desk and leaned forward. "Everybody does just that every day. First time I went surfing I'd never done it before. First time you did the storyboards for 'Fate Castle,' you'd never done it before."

"That's different," Brady muttered, raking one hand through his hair. He hadn't really looked at it like that, and, okay, Mike had a point. But those things weren't as important as a family, a kid, were they? "Screw up something like that, you get a do-over. Screw up your kid and it's forever."

"What makes you so sure you'd screw it up?"

Brady shook his head. Mike already knew why. At least, he knew enough of Brady's past that he never should have asked that question.

"You've got a shot at something here, Brady." Mike looked him in the eye and continued, "A woman who loves you, a baby who needs you. You've been trying to escape your past your whole life. Well, maybe it's time to stop running. Maybe it's time that you *make* the family that you missed out on."

Sounded so easy, and Brady knew it wasn't.

"How?" He really wanted to know. To think it could be done. Hope was a knife in his chest, sharp and slicing away at his doubts.

"The kind of family you wanted when you were a kid and never had?" Mike asked. "Build that. Build it now for Aine, your son—and yourself. Stop cheating yourself out of what you need and want and make a grab for it instead." He laughed a little and shook his head. "Go back to Ireland. Make the family you missed—before you miss this one, too."

Brady stared at him as hope continued to carve away at the black doubts that had been a part of him all his life. Was it possible? He thought back to when he was a kid and all the dreams he'd had about the kind of family he wanted. It was all there, in Ireland, waiting for him.

If Brady was willing to take the risk.

He took his first easy breath since leaving Aine and thought it all through again. Wasn't trying for something great and failing better than not trying at all? And when, he asked himself, had he *ever* failed when he wanted something badly enough? The answer was never. Why hadn't he remembered that? Hell, he thought, maybe all he really needed was a little faith. In himself. In Aine. In the kind of future he used to dream about.

"Mike," he said, already moving for the door, "I'm gonna need the company jet again."

"Yeah?" Mike grinned. "For how long?"

Brady stopped in the doorway and looked back over his shoulder at his friend. "Just long enough to get me to Ireland."

Mike's grin was even wider now. "So guess you'll be working long-distance from now on?"

"With any luck," Brady agreed. "With the internet and Skype and hell, the *phone*, I can work anywhere. And you guys will come out for the grand opening, right?"

"Wouldn't miss it," Mike said, and walked toward him, hand extended.

Brady took it, then yanked his friend in for a short hard hug. "Thanks, man. For everything."

Mike slapped Brady's shoulder. "We'll want an invite to the wedding, too."

"Count on it." Brady left to pack, then headed to the airport, hoping it wasn't too late.

"He'll be back, love," Molly told her daughter over a cup of tea.

Her mother's kitchen was warm and cozy despite the cold wind battering at the windows. Moonlight pearled on the glass and illuminated the surrounding trees with a pale silver glow. But inside, there was warm light and comfort.

"I don't think so." Aine hoped her mother was right, but when she remembered the stoic look of determination on Brady's features as he told her he couldn't be what she wanted, her heart ached.

Three days he'd been gone, and it felt as though nothing would ever be right in her world again. Three days and she could hardly take a step without thinking of him. How was she supposed to live the rest of her life without him?

"Why don't you move back here to the cottage for a while?" her mother asked, reaching out to take Aine's hand and give it a squeeze. "Truth be told, I could use the company, as I've hardly seen Robbie. Since Brady gave him that art program, the boy's been locked in his room creating all manner of horrible creatures from zombies to slavering hounds—" She broke off and sighed. "I'm sorry to mention his name, then, if it hurts you so."

"No," Aine said, forcing the smile her mother needed. "It's all right. I'm glad Robbie's enjoying the program, as Brady said he had real talent."

He'd even talked about offering Robbie a job once the boy finished school, and now Aine wondered if that promise would disappear. So much had changed with his leaving. She could hardly bring herself to care about the progress on the castle.

The roof tiles had finally arrived and were near to finished being laid. Soon the top floor would be renovated and then the hotel would be open for business. Would Brady come back for the opening?

"Thanks, Mum," Aine said softly. "But I'll stay at the castle still. It's worked out well, me being close at hand for Danny and the rest of the crew. And to be honest, I'm not really good company right now."

She didn't want comfort, no matter how well meant. She wanted to feel the pain of Brady's loss because it kept him near. She needed to be by herself, to get used to being alone. When she stood up, Molly joined her, coming around the kitchen table to envelop her in a hug.

Stroking her daughter's hair, she murmured, "There's always a chance for love, Aine. Never stop hoping. Never stop, because when you do, that's when all is lost."

Eleven

The second time he drove to the castle, Brady knew exactly where he was going.

To the only place he wanted to be.

Moonlight guided his way down the narrow curving track, past the iron gates now painted a bright silver and along the graveled drive. He spared a quick glance at the cottage where Molly and Robbie lived, but drove on to the main castle. It was a dark shadow against a moonlit sky and seemed to loom over him, daring him to step inside, to claim what he'd come for.

Brady was up to the challenge.

Finally, he was ready to leave his past behind and was ready now to reach for more. To take what he wanted, needed. He only hoped he could convince Aine that he was a changed man. That it was *she* who'd changed him. He used his key to open the front door, then quietly closed

and locked it behind him. The silence was all encompass-
ing and he did nothing to shatter it, taking the stairs with
hardly a breath of sound.

He turned on the landing and headed for her room,
praying she was still there and hadn't moved back to
the cottage. Her door wasn't locked, and he took that
as a good sign. Moving into the shadow-filled room, he
stopped at the foot of the wide bed and watched her sleeping. Moonlight was here, too, slanted across the bed,
making her dark red hair shine as it picked up threads of
gold in the auburn mass. She had one arm crooked behind
her head and the other cradling their child.

The heaviness in his chest that had been with him
for days lifted. His heart swelled as a rush of warmth
spread through him. Everything he wanted in life was
there, in that bed.

He stripped out of his clothes and gently eased into the
bed beside her. Brady pulled her to him and he marveled
to notice that she didn't wake up. Wasn't frightened. Instead, she curled into him, draping one arm across his
stomach, as if she'd only been lying there waiting for
him to touch her.

For the first time in days, Brady's heart lurched into
life and the sensation was almost painful.

The scent of her filled him; the warmth of her sighs
against his skin fired his blood as well as his soul. And
because he couldn't resist her another moment, he bent
his head and kissed her. Sleepily, she kissed him back,
sighing as she did so her breath became his, and then
she woke, opened her eyes, stared at him and whispered,
"Brady?"

When she would have pulled away, he only wrapped
his arms more tightly around her, holding her close, half-

afraid that if he let her go, she'd remain out of his reach forever. "Aine, I'm back. I'm here to stay, if you'll have me."

She looked up at him, not speaking, just watching him through those moss-green eyes. He didn't have a clue what she was thinking, feeling. This was a hell of a time for her to figure out how to mask her emotions. Worry pealed in his brain like warning bells going off.

Brady started talking, knowing that choosing the right words now was the most important thing he'd ever done. He wanted to be poetic. Romantic. He wanted to tell her that he wouldn't take no for an answer anymore. She was *going* to marry him. He wouldn't settle for less. Yet looking at her made him say only the simple truth. "I want to be here. With you. And I really need you to want me, too."

She opened her mouth to speak, but before she could, he spread one hand flat on her rounded belly and said, "I want to be a father to our baby. I want to be good at it, so I will be. I finally remembered that I've never failed at anything when I really want it. And I've never wanted anything like I want you and the family we can make."

At his words, he felt that small ripple of movement beneath his hands that told him his son was real and alive, and his heart filled even beyond what he would have thought possible.

"I want to live here in Ireland, with you. I can work from anywhere," he told her, words bursting from him as if they'd been dammed up behind a wall of stubbornness and had only just broken through. "We'll build our own house here, on the grounds. Behind the maze, maybe, I don't care. We'll be near your family, because they're almost as important to me as they are to you."

She swallowed hard and blinked back tears.

He hurried on, "I figure we can live here in the castle until the house is built. Any kind you want. We can build it to match the cottage, or even a replica of the castle itself if that's what you want."

She laughed a little, and he took that as hopeful. He had to keep talking because once he stopped she'd make her decision, and he needed to do what he could to make sure it was the *right* one.

"The house doesn't matter to me," he said. "What matters is the *home* we'll make in it."

Aine watched him, and in the moonlight, he could see the cautious hope in her gaze. When she spoke, her voice was soft, and the music that wove through it wrapped around his heart even as she shared her doubts.

"Though I'm so glad to see you, and I want you here more than anything," she said, "I've no wish to be a duty you carry through your life with brave resolution."

"You're not a duty," he interrupted her quickly, desperate now to make her see the truth he'd only realized. "You're a gift. You're the only truly great gift I've ever been blessed with. I don't know what I did to earn you coming into my life, but I'm grateful."

"Brady..." She chewed at her bottom lip and he saw the first glimmer of tears in her eyes. Not sure if they were happy or sad tears, he rushed on, fighting now for the life he'd always wanted. The life that was just out of reach.

"I made myself into what I am," he said, stroking her hair back from her face with his fingertips. "And I did a good job of it. But with you, I'm *more* than I ever thought I could be. With you, I have everything. Without you, there's *nothing*. It's really just that simple, Aine. You're my heart. Without you I'm only half-alive."

Her mouth curved the slightest bit as she reached to cup his cheek in her palm. "And the words, Brady? I told you I wanted the words. And the promise of them."

"I'll give you the promise," he said, and reached around to the bedside table where he'd left the ring he'd carried in his pocket all the way from California. He'd bought it on his way to the airport and had kept it close to him, like a talisman, like the promise she was waiting for. Holding the square-cut emerald that had reminded him of her, he looked from it to her and knew that no gem could ever shine with the beauty and depth of her eyes.

"I want you to marry me, Aine," he said, voice low and steady. "Not for the baby. Not for duty. But because with you I found something I never really believed in." He took a breath, blew it out and grinned at her. "*I love you*. Never thought I'd say those words. Never thought I'd need to say those words. But I do. I want to say them to you for the rest of my life. *I love you, Aine*. I promise you I always will."

Her smile was wide and bright and filled with everything he'd flown thousands of miles hoping to see.

"I'll marry you, Brady Finn, for I love you so much," she whispered, and held out her hand for him to slide the ring home. "I promise you I always will."

"Thank God," he muttered, and dropped his forehead to hers.

She laid one hand atop his so that both of them were cradling the child they'd made, connecting the three of them into a unit.

"I swear," he said softly, kissing her once, twice, "I will never take for granted the family we'll make together."

She laughed, hooked her arm around his neck and

brought him close enough for a long, deep kiss. "And what a family we'll make, my love." She kissed him again and he felt all the love she held for him rush through him, filling all of the dark, empty places inside him.

With Aine curled against him in the moonlight, Brady finally felt like a rich man.

Epilogue

The grand reopening of Fate Castle emptied the village and half the county. They weren't accepting paying guests until the new year, giving Brady and Aine a chance to settle into marriage without zombie hunters underfoot all the time. But having the renovations complete made them want to show the locals just what they'd done to the place. So far, people liked it.

October was too cold to hold the party outside, so the medieval banquet hall was being christened. There was traditional Irish music that had people up and dancing, tables groaned under a mountain of food and there was enough beer to fill a moat, if the castle had had one.

Brady watched the celebration and told himself again that he was a lucky man. He'd found where he belonged. He had a beautiful wife who loved him, and a son on the way, not to mention a mother-in-law and a younger brother. He'd come here to build a hotel and had instead found the kind of life he used to dream of.

Long-distance working was going fine, too. With weekly Skype meetings, not to mention innumerable phone calls with either Sean or Mike, he kept up with everything. His own work had been going better than ever. Maybe, he thought, it was all the atmosphere at the castle, but he'd come up with some great story lines for future games.

And Robbie, Brady thought as he spotted the boy across the hall talking to Celia Hannigan, had been a big help. The kid was talented and eager to start working for Celtic Knot. But now that he was in the big-brother position, Brady was also insisting the kid go to college. Robbie'd work part-time and get real-world experience while learning as much as he could about graphic design.

Molly was supervising the food tables, making sure everyone had plenty to eat. The woman was never happier than in a kitchen, and Brady loved being able to pop into the cottage for tea and some of her amazing cookies whenever he wanted to.

Aine caught Brady's eye as she danced with Sean Ryan. One look at his amazing wife and his heart gave an oh-so-familiar jolt. He doubted he'd ever get past the rush he felt just knowing she was his.

"You look happy."

Brady glanced at Mike Ryan as he stepped up and handed over a pint glass of Guinness. "That's because I am."

"The hotel turned out great," Mike said, sweeping his gaze across the pennants and tapestries on the walls. There were suits of armor in the corners of the room and pewter plates and mugs scattered across the long tables. "I think it's going to be a winner."

"With the web contest we'll be running after the first of the year, you can bet on it," Brady said. "And Aine's getting emails every day from fans of the game wanting to make reservations even though we're not officially open yet."

"Good to know," Mike said. "Oh, we got the final papers on the river hotel last week. We're set to go there for the River Haunt."

"That's great, and before I forget," Brady said, pausing for a sip of his beer, "I got an email from Jenny Marshall with the new drawings she's come up with for the River Haunt hotel."

Mike gritted his teeth. "Yeah?"

Brady laughed at Mike's resigned expression. "What is it with you and her?"

"Nothing." Mike shook his head, brushing off the question. "I already told you. We met, then we said good-bye."

"Yeah, you're a master storyteller," Brady said wryly, then added, "Well, you'd better get over whatever your issue with her is since you'll be working together on the hotel."

"We'll see," Mike muttered. "I'm thinking Joe would do a better job of the murals."

"Joe quit, bud. How do you not know that?" Brady looked at him. "I live in *Ireland* and I know he quit two weeks ago."

"Perfect," Mike grumbled. "Just freaking perfect."

"Relax. Maybe your hotel project will work out as well for you as mine did for me."

"No chance of that if Jenny Marshall's involved," Mike

told him, then smiled and changed the subject. "Enough about the thorn in my side. Here comes your beautiful wife, you lucky bastard."

Brady turned to grin at the woman walking toward him with green eyes shining and a smile curving her delectable mouth. She looked amazing in black pants and a dark red sweater that did nothing to disguise her growing belly. Her hair was loose and curled around her shoulders, her cheeks were flushed and those eyes were sparkling.

"Mike, do you mind? My new husband promised to dance with me tonight, and I've come to hold him to it."

"Just as long as you save one for me, too," Mike said.

"A deal, it is," Aine told him, then threaded her arm through Brady's as they walked to the middle of the floor. The castle was alive with light and color, and the party was a huge success. She'd already had dozens of people say they wanted to come and stay as soon as they were open. Apparently the locals loved the idea of a werewolf chase through the maze!

Brady covered her hand with his as they walked, and the pulse of heat from his touch dazzled her. She supposed it always would. And wasn't that a wonderful thing? Aine hugged her happiness close, smiling at her friends and family as she and Brady strolled to the dance floor.

The musicians slid from a toe-tapping reel into a slow, soft tune that sailed over the heads of everyone gathered and hung in the air like a sigh.

"Have I told you tonight how gorgeous you are?" Brady asked as he guided her into a slow, lazy circle.

"You have," she said, trailing her fingertips through his hair, loving the silky touch of it against her skin. "And have I told you that I love you?"

"You have, but don't let that stop you from saying it again," he said, smiling, then dipped his head down to claim a kiss.

Magic had happened, Aine thought, looking up into her husband's eyes and seeing love shine back at her. The castle she'd fought to protect was safe, the man she loved had come home to her and the child they'd made was healthy. Her mother had her home, her brother had a future and she and Brady had everything. Her baby gave a quick kick as if sharing the joy she felt.

"Then, let me say it again, every day." She cupped his cheek in her palm. "I love you, Brady Finn. Now and always."

He grinned and spun her around, making the colors and people around them swirl into a blur. She felt as if they were the only two people in the world.

Aine laid her head on his chest and as the music wove its spell around them, they danced into the future.

* * * * *

*If you loved this novel, pick up these other stories of
pregnancy and romance from
USA TODAY bestselling author Maureen Child*

*HIGH-SOCIETY SECRET PREGNANCY
AFTER HOURS WITH HER EX*

Available now from Harlequin Desire!

*Look for Mike and Jenny's story,
coming December 2015,
only from USA TODAY bestselling author
Maureen Child and Harlequin Desire!*

*If you're on Twitter, tell us what you think
of Harlequin Desire! #harlequindesire*

REQUEST YOUR FREE BOOKS!
2 FREE NOVELS PLUS 2 FREE GIFTS!

(H) HARLEQUIN®

Desire

ALWAYS POWERFUL, PASSIONATE AND PROVOCATIVE

YES! Please send me 2 FREE Harlequin® Desire novels and my 2 FREE gifts (gifts are worth about $10). After receiving them, if I don't wish to receive any more books, I can return the shipping statement marked "cancel." If I don't cancel, I will receive 6 brand-new novels every month and be billed just $4.55 per book in the U.S. or $5.24 per book in Canada. That's a savings of at least 13% off the cover price! It's quite a bargain! Shipping and handling is just 50¢ per book in the U.S. and 75¢ per book in Canada.* I understand that accepting the 2 free books and gifts places me under no obligation to buy anything. I can always return a shipment and cancel at any time. Even if I never buy another book, the two free books and gifts are mine to keep forever.

225/326 HDN GH2P

Name	(PLEASE PRINT)

Address	Apt. #

City	State/Prov.	Zip/Postal Code

Signature (if under 18, a parent or guardian must sign)

Mail to the **Reader Service:**
IN U.S.A.: P.O. Box 1867, Buffalo, NY 14240-1867
IN CANADA: P.O. Box 609, Fort Erie, Ontario L2A 5X3

Want to try two free books from another line?
Call 1-800-873-8635 or visit www.ReaderService.com.

* Terms and prices subject to change without notice. Prices do not include applicable taxes. Sales tax applicable in N.Y. Canadian residents will be charged applicable taxes. Offer not valid in Quebec. This offer is limited to one order per household. Not valid for current subscribers to Harlequin Desire books. All orders subject to credit approval. Credit or debit balances in a customer's account(s) may be offset by any other outstanding balance owed by or to the customer. Please allow 4 to 6 weeks for delivery. Offer available while quantities last.

Your Privacy—The Reader Service is committed to protecting your privacy. Our Privacy Policy is available online at www.ReaderService.com or upon request from the Reader Service.

We make a portion of our mailing list available to reputable third parties that offer products we believe may interest you. If you prefer that we not exchange your name with third parties, or if you wish to clarify or modify your communication preferences, please visit us at www.ReaderService.com/consumerschoice or write to us at Reader Service Preference Service, P.O. Box 9062, Buffalo, NY 14240-9062. Include your complete name and address.

Isabella was somehow even more beautiful than he'd
remembered. And probably more treacherous, Marc
reminded himself as he fought for control.

It had been six years since he'd seen her.

Six years since he'd held her, kissed her, made love
to her.

Six years since he'd kicked her out of his apartment
and his life.

And still, he wanted her.

It came as something of a shock, considering he'd
done his best not to think about her in the ensuing years.

All it had taken was a glimpse of her gorgeous red hair,
her warm brown eyes, from the small window embedded
in the classroom door to throw him right back into the
seething, tumultuous heat that had characterized so much
of their relationship. He hadn't cared about anything
but getting into that room to see if his mind was playing
tricks on him.

Six years ago he had kicked Isa Varin—now, apparently,
Isabella Moreno—out of his life in the cruelest manner
possible. He didn't regret making her leave—how could

he when she'd betrayed him so completely?—but in the time since, he had regretted how he'd done it. When he'd come to his senses and sent his driver to find her and deliver her things, including her purse and cell phone and some money, she had vanished into thin air. He'd looked for her, but he'd never found her.

Now he knew why. The very passionate, very beautiful, very bewitching Isa Varin had ceased to exist. In her place was this buttoned-down professor, her voice and face as cool and sharp as any diamond his mines had ever produced. Only the hair—that glorious red hair—was the same. Isabella Moreno wore it in a tight braid down her back instead of in the wild curls favored by his Isa, but he would know the color anywhere.

Black cherries at midnight.

Wet garnets shining in the filtered light of a full moon.

And when her eyes had met his over the heads of her students, he'd felt a punch in his gut—in his groin—that couldn't be denied. Only Isa had ever made his body react so powerfully.

One look into her eyes used to bring him to his knees. But those days were long gone. Her betrayal had destroyed any faith he might have had in her. He'd been weak once, had fallen for the innocence she could project with a look, a touch, a whisper.

He wouldn't make that mistake again.

Will Marc have Isa back in his bed, trust be damned?

Find out in CLAIMED, the first of the DIAMOND TYCOONS duet by New York Times bestselling author Tracy Wolff, available wherever Harlequin® Desire books and ebooks are sold.

www.Harlequin.com

Love the Harlequin book you just read?

Your opinion matters.

Review this book on your favorite book site, review site, blog or your own social media properties and share your opinion with other readers!

Be sure to connect with us at:
Harlequin.com/Newsletters
Facebook.com/HarlequinBooks
Twitter.com/HarlequinBooks

JUST CAN'T GET ENOUGH?

Join our social communities
and talk to us online.

You will have access to the latest
news on upcoming titles and special
promotions, but most importantly,
you can talk to other fans about your
favorite Harlequin reads.

Harlequin.com/Community

Facebook.com/HarlequinBooks

Twitter.com/HarlequinBooks

Pinterest.com/HarlequinBooks

THE WORLD IS BETTER WITH

Romance

Harlequin has everything from contemporary, passionate and heartwarming to suspenseful and inspirational stories.

Whatever your mood, we have a romance just for you!

Connect with us to find your next great read, special offers and more.

⧫ HARLEQUIN®

A *Romance* FOR EVERY MOOD™